Mãn

KIM THÚY

Mãn

Translated from the French by SHEILA FISCHMAN

Random House Canada

PUBLISHED BY RANDOM HOUSE CANADA

Copyright © 2013 Éditions Libre Expression
English Translation Copyright @ 2014 Sheila Fischman
Published by arrangement Group Librex, Montréal, Quebec, Canada

www.randomhouse.ca

Random House Canada and colophon are registered trademarks.

LIBRARY AND ARCHIVES CANADA CATALOGUING IN PUBLICATION

Thúy, Kim
[Mãn. English]
    Mãn / Kim Thúy ; translated by Sheila Fischman.

Translation of French book with same title.
Issued in print and electronic formats.

ISBN 978-0-345-81379-4
eBook ISBN 978-0-345-81381-7

1. Thúy, Kim—Fiction. I. Fischman, Sheila, translator
II. Title. III. Title: Mãn. English

PS8639.H89M3613 2014   c843'.6   c2014-900580-6

Cover and text design by CS Richardson
Cover image: © Dan Goldberg / Photographer's Choice / Getty Images
Interior image: © Jiri Hera / Shutterstock.com

Printed and bound in the United States of America

10 9 8 7 6 5 4 3 2 1

MAMAN AND I DON'T look like one another. She is short, I am tall. Her complexion is dark, my skin is like a French doll's. She has a hole in her calf and I have a hole in my heart.

My first mother, the one who conceived me and gave birth to me, had a hole in her head. She was a young adult or maybe still a little girl, for no Vietnamese woman would have dared carry a child unless she had a ring on her finger.

My second mother, the one who plucked me out of a vegetable garden among the okra, had a hole in her faith. She no longer believed in people, especially when they talked. And so she retired to a straw hut, far from the powerful arms of the Mekong, to recite prayers in Sanskrit.

My third mother, the one who watched me attempt my first steps, became Maman, my Maman. That morning, she wanted to open her arms again. And so she opened the shutters in her bedroom, which until that day had always been closed. In the distance, in the warm light, she saw me, and I became her daughter. She gave me a second birth by bringing me up in a big city, an anonymous else-where, behind a schoolyard, surrounded by children who envied me for having a mother who taught school and sold iced bananas.

VERY EARLY EVERY MORNING, before classes started, we went grocery shopping. We started with the woman who sold ripe coconuts, rich in flesh and poor in juice. The lady grated the first half-coconut with the cap of a soft drink bottle nailed to the end of a flat stick. Long strips fell in a decorative frieze, like ribbons, on the banana leaf spread out on the stall. The merchant talked non-stop and kept asking Maman the same question: "What do you feed that child to give her such red lips?" To avoid that question, I got in the habit of pressing my lips together, but I was so fascinated by how quickly she grated the second half that I always watched her with my mouth partly open. She set her foot on a long black metal spatula that had part of its handle sitting on a small wooden bench. Without looking at the pointed teeth at the rounded end of the spatula, she crumbled the nut at the speed of a machine.

The fall of the crumbs through the hole in the spatula must just resemble the flight of snowflakes in Santa Claus country, Maman always said, which was actually something her own mother would say. She spoke her mother's words to hear her voice again. And whenever she saw boys playing soccer with an empty tin can, she couldn't help but whisper *londi*, in her mother's voice.

THAT WAS MY FIRST word of French: *londi*. In
Vietnamese, *lon* means "tin can" and *đi*, "to go away."
In French, the two sounds together create *lundi* in the
ear of a Vietnamese woman. Following her own
mother's example, she taught me the French word by
asking me to point to the tin can then kick it, saying
lon đi for *lundi*. So that second day of the week is the
most beautiful of all for Maman because her mother
died before teaching her how to pronounce the other
days. Only *lundi* was associated with a clear, unforget-
table image. The other six days were absent from any
reference, therefore all alike. That's why my mother
often confused *mardi* with *jeudi* and sometimes
reversed *samedi* and *mercredi*.

thứ 2

~

lundi

thứ 3

~

mardi

thứ 4

~

mercredi

thứ 5

~

jeudi

thứ 6

~

vendredi

thứ 7

~

samedi

chủ nhật

~

dimanche

BEFORE HER MOTHER DIED, though, she'd had time to learn how to extract the milk from a coconut by squeezing chunks of crumbled flesh saturated with hot water. When mothers taught their daughters how to cook, they spoke in hushed tones, whispering so that neighbours couldn't steal recipes and possibly seduce their husbands with the same dishes. Culinary traditions are passed on secretly, like magic tricks between master and apprentice, one movement at a time, following the rhythms of each day. In the natural order, then, girls learned to measure the amount of water for cooking rice with the first joint of the index finger, to cut "vicious peppers" (*ớt hiểm*) with the point of the knife to transform them into harmless flowers, to peel mangoes from base to stem so they won't go against the direction of the fibres . . .

THAT WAS HOW I LEARNED from my mother that
of the dozens of kinds of bananas sold at the market,
only the *chuối xiêm* could be flattened without being
crushed and frozen without turning black. When I
first came to Montreal, I prepared it as a treat for my
husband, who hadn't eaten it for twenty years. I
wanted him to taste once again the typical marriage of
peanuts and coconut, two ingredients that in south
Vietnam are served as much at dessert as at breakfast.
I hoped to be able to serve and be a companion to my
husband without disturbing anything, a little like
flavours that are hardly noticed because they are
ever-present.

chuối

~

banana

chồng

~

husband

MAMAN ENTRUSTED ME TO this man out of motherly love, just as the nun, my second mother, had given me to her, thinking about my future. Because Maman was preparing for her death, knowing that one day she would no longer be around, she sought a husband for me who would have the qualities of a father. One of her friends, acting as matchmaker, brought him to visit us one afternoon. Maman asked me to serve the tea, that was all. I did not look at the face of the man even when I set the cup in front of him. My gaze wasn't required, it was only his that mattered.

HE HAD COME FROM FAR AWAY and didn't have
much time. Several families were waiting to introduce
him to their daughters. He was from Saigon but had
left Vietnam at twenty, as one of the boat people. He
had spent several years in a refugee camp in Thailand
before coming to Montreal, where he'd found work
but not exactly a home. He was one of those who had
lived too long in Vietnam to become Canadian. And
conversely, who have lived too long in Canada to be
Vietnamese again.

thuyền nhân

~

boat people

WHEN HE GOT UP from our table, his steps to the door were uncertain, like those of a man lost between two worlds. He no longer knew if he was supposed to cross the threshold before or after a woman. He no longer knew if his words should be those of the matchmaker or his own. His flubs when he spoke to Maman stunned us all. He called her, at random, Big Sister (*Chị*), Aunt (*Cô*) and Great-Aunt (*Bác*). No one held it against him that he came from elsewhere, from a place where personal pronouns exist so that they can remain impersonal. In the absence of those pronouns, the Vietnamese language imposes a relationship from the very first contact: the younger of the two interlocutors must respect and obey the elder, and conversely, the elder must give advice and protection to the younger. If someone were to listen to a conversation between them, he would be able to guess that, for example, the younger one is the nephew of one of his mother's older brothers. Similarly, if the conversation were taking place between two people with no family ties, it would be possible as well to determine whether the elder is younger than the parents of the other. In the case of my future husband, he might have partially expressed his interest in me if he'd called Maman *Bác*, because Great-Aunt would have elevated Maman to the rank of his parents and would have implied her position of mother-in-law. But uncertainty had mixed him up.

TO OUR AMAZEMENT, he came back the following   *quạt máy*
day with offerings: a fan, a box of maple cookies and a   ~
bottle of shampoo. This time, I was obliged to sit   fan
between Maman and the matchmaker, across from
the man and his parents, who were making a display
on the table of photos that showed him at the wheel of
his car, standing in front of some tulips, and in his
restaurant holding two big bowls with his thumb
nearly touching the scalding broth. Lots of photos of
him, always alone.

MAMAN AGREED TO A third visit two days later. He
asked for some time alone with me. In Vietnam, cafés
with their chairs facing the street, like in France, were
intended for men. Girls without makeup or false
eyelashes didn't drink coffee, at least not in public. We
could have had smoothies with soursop, sapodilla or
papaya at the place next door, but that patch of garden
with its blue plastic stools seemed reserved for the
veiled smiles of schoolgirls and the timid touches of
young lovers' hands. Whereas we were merely future
spouses. Of the whole neighbourhood, all that was left
to us was the pink granite bench in front of the row of
apartments for the teachers, including ours, in the
schoolyard, under the poinciana tree heavy with
flowers but with branches as delicate and graceful as a
ballerina's arms. Bright red petals covered the whole
bench until he cleared part of it so he could sit down. I
remained standing to look at him and regretted that
he couldn't see himself surrounded by all those
flowers. At that precise moment, I knew that I would
always remain standing, that he would never think of
making room for me beside him because that was the
sort of man he was, alone and lonely.

I OFFERED HIM THE glass of lemonade with salt   *con sóc*
lime that my mother had prepared for him. He   ~
reminded me of those brown limes marinated in salt,   squirrel
warmed in the sun and altered completely by time, for
his eyes were not old but aged, almost blurred, faded.

"Have you ever seen a squirrel?"
"Just in books."
"I'm leaving tomorrow."
Silence.
"I'll send you the papers."
Silence.
"We'll have children."
"Yes."

He gave me his address and phone number on a
sheet of paper folded in two. He left, walking slowly
and unobtrusively like the soldier who had given
Maman this poem, also written on a page folded in two:

Anh tặng em
Cuộc đời anh không sống
Giấc mơ anh chỉ mơ
Một tâm hồn để trống
Những đêm trắng mong chờ

Anh tặng em
Bài thơ anh không viết
Nỗi đau anh đi tìm

Màu mây anh chưa biết
Tha thiết của lặng im

I offer you
The life I have not lived
The dream I can but dream
A soul I've left empty
During sleepless nights

As I go to you I hold as an offering
The poem I have not written
The ache towards which I strain
The colour of the cloud I haven't known
The longings of silence.

HIS NAME WAS PHƯƠNG. Maman had known him
since he'd started playing a version of pétanque,
bowling with sandals instead of steel balls. She noticed
him because he always missed his shot when she
passed by him on the way home from school. His
teammates said that Maman brought him bad luck.
As for him, he waited for his chance every day at the
same time, even if he did not yet know what he was
waiting for. He was able to give a precise name to that
expectation only when he saw her arrive for the first
time in a white *áo dài*, the uniform of her new school,
whose name was embroidered in blue on a label sewn
between her shoulder and her left breast. In the
distance, the panels of her tunic blowing in the wind
transformed her into a butterfly in gentle flight,
destination unknown. From that precise moment, he
never missed a single outing of Maman's class and he
followed her, keeping his distance, to her home.

áo dài

~

tunic

guốc

~

wooden sandals

with heels

HE SPOKE TO HER for the first time long afterwards, when the heel of Maman's shoe broke, as her half-brothers and half-sisters had predicted would happen. He rushed to her spontaneously to offer her his own sandals, then took off with the broken-heeled shoe. He was surprised to observe saw marks in the wood when he tried to repair it in the workshop of a cousin who made coffins. The next day, he was waiting for her in front of the bougainvillea that gave a softening effect to the strict metal of the front door of the judge's house. As soon as he saw Maman's foot on the first paving stone of the path, he bent down to place the shoes in the right direction on the threshold. To avoid compromising Maman's reputation, he stepped away a few metres. She slipped them on and then, in turn, placed in her own footprints Phương's sandals, the ones that had let her continue home without getting dirty, without stopping, without crying.

EVER SINCE PHƯƠNG'S SHADOW had been follow-   *mưa*
ing hers, she'd stopped crying under her umbrella,   ~
which had been pierced with a needle and looked   rain
like a sieve, because Phương's was always there to
protect her before the first drop fell and even before
Maman had caught sight of the first grey cloud. And
so she carried two umbrellas, one beneath the other,
and Phương, bare-headed, walked three paces behind
her. He had never wanted to take shelter under the
same one because with the two of them, the rain
could have dulled the lustre of Maman's perfectly
smooth black hair.

From outside the garden planted with longan,
papaya and jackfruit trees, it was impossible to hear
Maman's silence. No one aside from the servants
could have imagined that her half-brothers and
half-sisters made a game of breaking every other tooth
in her comb and cutting locks of her hair while she
slept. Maman was able to convince herself of the
innocence of their acts, or the fact that the acts flowed
from their very innocence. She remained silent to
preserve that innocence as well as her father's. She did
not want her father to see his own children tear one
another to pieces, for already he was both witness and
judge of the ripping apart of his country, its culture,
its people.

HER FATHER WOULD HAVE preferred not to have
children with a second wife after the sudden death of
the first, for that new spouse would inevitably become
a *Mẹ Ghẻ*—a "cold mother." However, he did not yet
have a son who would ensure the continuity of his
own father's family name and that of all the ancestors
who watched over him and carried him from the top
of their altar. And so that cold mother played her role
as spouse by giving him sons, and the role of parent in
the manner of the stepmothers of Snow White,
Cinderella and all the other orphaned princesses.

It should be said that *ghẻ* also means "mange." And
so, to live up to the ugly title "mangy mother" that
had been inflicted on her, she showed her children
how to hate Maman and her big sisters, how to draw
the line between the first and second litter, how to
differentiate oneself from those other girls even
though they all had the same nose. I wonder if that
mangy mother would have been less bitter had she
been called *stepmother*. Would she have been less
afraid of the beauty of Maman's big sisters? Would
she have been less eager to marry them off?

BEING YOUNGER, Maman awaited her turn to be
given in marriage separating the stone and gravel
fragments from the rice like prayer beads. Her cold
mother forbade the cooks to help her so she would
learn obedience and discipline. And so what she
learned above all was how to become flexible, imper-
ceptible, invisible even. When her mother died, people
told her that she'd gone because she had finished
paying her debts on earth. So then Maman discarded
stones as if they were part of her debt, a weight that
prevented her from taking flight. She got rid of them
in the hope of arriving at the state of weightlessness.
She was thrilled to see her jar fill up with those
impurities meal after meal, day after day. She buried
the jar under the mango tree next to the cookie tin
that held *Une vie*, by Guy de Maupassant, a book from
her mother's library that she'd been able to save. Her
cold mother needed space on the shelf for the wind to
circulate around the hammock. She may have been
right, because the length of cloth that hung from the
ceiling functioned as a fan, moving the air just above
her husband's sleeping body.

IT WAS UP TO MAMAN to pull the cord that made the fan move from left to right at a steady rhythm so as to drive away the heat without interrupting her father's siesta. Maman loved that special moment with him; she was certain that the gentle, repetitive movement reassured him, confirmed that family harmony existed.

Sometimes, when he was so preoccupied he couldn't sleep, he would ask her to recite *Truyện Kiều*, the story of a girl who sacrificed herself to save her family. Some say that as long as the poem, with its more than three thousand lines, still exists, no war can make Vietnam disappear. Maybe that is why, for more than a century, even an illiterate Vietnamese has been able to recite entire stanzas.

Maman's father demanded that all his children learn the poem by heart, because in it the poet depicted, among other things, purity and selflessness, two shades essential to the Vietnamese soul. As for Maman's mother, she always came back to the first lines of the poem, which remind the reader that everything can change, everything can topple in the blink of an eye.

One hundred years, span of a human life,
A combat zone where fate and talent clash, ruthless
The ocean roars where brambles once grew
In this world the spectacle clutches your heart.

Why be surprised? Nothing is given without compensation.

The blue sky often rains its curses on beauties with pink cheeks.

MAMAN SAW HER LIFE turned upside down when the first shot was heard in an ambush between two shores, between East and West, between the resistance clamouring for independence and the current regime that taught Vietnamese students to say "our ancestors the Gauls" without seeing any inconsistency. She was on one of the Mekong ferry boats when the first bullets struck passengers. Everyone fell and took cover instinctively. And instinctively, she raised her head during the first silence as preparations were being made for the second burst of fire. Her neighbour, an elderly man with missing teeth, leathery skin and bright eyes, looked down as he ordered her to throw all her papers overboard: "If you want to survive, get rid of your identity."

AFTERWARDS, CHAOS. Children sobbing as they
begged their parents to wake up, hens clucking and
struggling in their wicker baskets, objects falling then
landing and gliding from left to right and right to left
became entangled to create the cacophonous melody
typical of panic in the face of the unknown and, even
more, the known. The conflicts lay in the cracks of
normality. They breathed the same air as the girls
skipping rope and they shared the spaces of the boys
who were playing at cricket fights. People learned to
give money to government officials by day and rice to
the partisans by night. They crept between two lines
of fire, careful not to set foot on one boundary or the
other, invisible and changing depending on the time.
They remained neutral by embracing both, like a
father who loves his two warring sons.

Maman, without identity papers, could go on being
neutral when armed men told her to get up and follow
them. She took only three steps before fainting
because she had seen her white tunic coloured with
blood-red stains. She thought she'd been hit, but it was
the blood of other passengers, including the neighbour
who had been impassive in the face of orders given at
the butts of rifles and the barrels of guns.

hai làng đạn

~

two lines
of fire

MAMAN WOKE UP IN the corner of a straw hut, surrounded by familiar sounds. Nearby, crackling coals, the rustling of water palms and the whispering of discussions were punctuated by the yapping of dogs and the steady whack of a knife on a plank of wood. The scent of chopped lemongrass caressed her nostrils like a mother's hand on her cheek. In this way, she stopped being afraid. Still, she opened her eyes on a world that was strange and unknown to her. In the village, there were no longer "women" or "men," no "aunts" or "great-uncles," only comrades. She became Comrade Nhẫn, a name she gave herself before opening her eyes for the first time, a name that had no baggage and no family. The name came to her almost naturally because she'd repeated it hundreds of times over basins of her brothers' and sisters' soiled laundry. At each of the spots and dirty marks they'd made deliberately to spoil the whiteness of the white cotton and to challenge the effectiveness of 72 percent soap like that from Marseille, she said very softly, "*kiên nhẫn*"—"patience"—her personal mantra, or rather her personal accomplishment, because she was finally able to hear the gently captivating melody created by the rubbing of wet and soapy cloth.

For five years she lived in this village as Nhẫn, a name that carried a message, like all the others. Some had chosen Determination (*Chí*). Others had preferred Fatherland (*Quốc*), and still others had dared to pick Courage (*Dũng*) or Peace (*Bình*). All had given up Orchid (*Lan*), Prosperity (*Lộc*) and Snow (*Tuyết*).

Perhaps she could have escaped and gone home, because there were neither fences nor barbed wire around the village. No one had tortured her. No one had tied her down. No one had interrogated her. What they demanded was simply some essays and presentations on patriotism, courage, independence, colonialism, sacrifice. They hadn't asked for her parents' names, the number of her brothers and sisters, and, most important, never asked for her real name, because members of the resistance had left their families for a collective cause that overshadowed their individual lives. Unlike her, most had joined the resistance of their own free will. She was ashamed of never having felt the same unconditional love for this country which was hers as well. She was ashamed of wanting to stay within the invisible boundaries because she wanted to spare her family suspicions and accusations of treason if she went back to settle with them after living on the other shore, on enemy land. She stayed there for herself as well, to avoid living. In the village, she just had to follow.

AT FIRST, SHE FOLLOWED the routine of those in charge of the kitchen and the health care group. Later, once her feet were protected by calluses and toughened scars, she would walk for weeks to translate chemistry textbooks from French to Vietnamese for workers who manufactured mines in the heart of the tropical forest. One day, she received an order to follow a female comrade wearing a brown Vietnamese shirt. She took Maman to the market, where a woman dressed in a faded lavender-coloured smock gave her a yoke. At one end, the basket contained Chinese water spinach, at the other, yams. Those enormous roots made the yoke tip back when she hoisted the bamboo carrying pole onto her shoulder. Maman lost her balance in the first seconds before she learned how to synchronize the rhythm of the two weights with her steps. She crossed the checkpoint on the bridge by blending into the crowd. A few streets from the bridge exit, she lost sight of the woman in the lavender smock. But a little farther along, another woman called out to her, grabbing her arm.

"Little sister, are your yams nice and starchy today? They look good to me. My son just had a tooth pulled. I want to make him some yam soup as a change from rice soup. He's a fussy one. But he's a good boy! I really don't like grating yams. It always makes my hands sting. Can you help me? Can you come to the house and grate them for me? Come! Come with me."

By following the woman, she was starting, unwittingly, her work as a spy for the resistance.

SHE SLEPT IN THE woman's kitchen for several weeks, then was moved to another house where she might prove useful. During the journey, which took her through a durian plantation, in the midst of those heavy, prickly fruit that fortunately fall only at night, she spotted her father in conversation with two men. She felt a spontaneous urge to run towards him as she used to do when she was a little girl. Her guide saw Maman's conical hat slip towards her back, revealing her eyes, which betrayed her impulse. Before she could turn her body in the same direction as her eyes, Maman heard: "*Đừng*." The guide did not say "No" or "Stop" or "Walk," but "Restrain yourself." Maman looked away. Her father seemed to have aged a great deal in five years. He still had the imposing posture of a judge, but his cheeks sagged now as if they'd lost the muscles for smiling. She was afraid he would see her because that would give him one more burden to carry, one more situation to resolve and, above all, hundreds of answers to give to the authorities.

It was the last time Maman saw her father: beneath the durians, which the Vietnamese call *sầu riêng*. Until that day, she had never thought about the name formed by those two words, which means literally "personal sorrows." One forgets perhaps that those sorrows, like their flesh, are sealed hermetically into compartments under a carapace bristling with thorns.

AS FOR ME, I never knew who my father was.   *trắng*
Mean-spirited gossips suspect that he is white, tall   ~
and a colonizer because I have a delicate nose and   white
luminous, pale skin. Maman often told me she'd
always wanted that whiteness for me; the whiteness
of *bánh cuốn*. She would take me to the vendor of
Vietnamese crepes to watch her spread the rice flour
mixture onto a piece of heavy cotton placed directly
above a gigantic cauldron of boiling water. She spread
the liquid by turning her ladle onto the cloth to cover
it completely. In a few seconds, the cream was transformed into a thin, translucent skin that she would
peel off with a bamboo stalk sharpened into a long,
thin paddle. Maman claimed that she was the only
mother who knew how to wrap her daughter in that
crepe while she was napping so that her skin could be
compared with the shimmer of snow and the bril-
liance of porcelain. In the same way the lotuses
preserve their perfume despite the stench of the
swamps where they grow, I must never allow rude
comments to soil that purity.

Maman also knew the secret of how to change the
shape of the nose. Some Asian women try to increase
the prominence of their nasal bones with silicone
implants, but Maman just had to gently pull my nose
nine times every morning to Westernize it. That's
why my name is Mān, which means "perfectly
fulfilled," or "may there be nothing left to desire," or
"may all wishes be granted." I can ask for nothing

more because my name imposes on me that state of satisfaction and satiety. Unlike Guy de Maupassant's Jeanne, who dreamed of grasping all the joys in life when she left the convent, I grew up without dreams.

MAMAN HAD BEEN ABLE to create a peaceful life
for us between two worlds. I found that divided
space again in Montreal, in my husband's restaurant
kitchen. The movements of life outside were kept
on hold by the constant noise of the exhaust fan.
Time was marked by the number of orders inserted
in the slit of the metal bar and not by minutes or
hours. In summer, it was the relentless heat that
distorted the very notion of time. In winter, the fire
door that opened onto the yard was permanently
closed, turning the kitchen into a strongbox. The man
who cleaned the filters in the exhaust fan was the only
person who brought back some life to the space. He
came once a month. He always knocked very loudly,
as if he were in distress—though he was in a hurry
only because his long list of clients demanded speed
and his wife, clean hands with no oil. He was the one
who taught me to use the weather as a greeting.

"Nice day."
"It's hot."
"It's hailing."
"It's snowing."
"It's windy."
"It's raining."

IN SOUTH VIETNAM, we never talk about the weather. We never make comments, perhaps because there are no seasons, no changes, like in this kitchen. Or maybe because we accept things as they are, as they happen to us, never asking why or how.

Once, through the little square opening for serving the plates, I heard some lawyer clients say that you should only ask questions to which you already know the answers. Otherwise, it's better to be silent. I will never find answers to my questions, and that may be why I've never asked one. All I did was climb up and down the stairs that connected my oven to my bed. My husband built the stairwell to protect me from the cold in winter and the vagaries of life outside in any weather.

WHEN I FIRST ARRIVED, the restaurant menu was
very basic, like those in street restaurants in Vietnam:
one dish, one specialty. In Hanoi, the old district was
criss-crossed by streets that specialized in a single
product: Vermicelli Street, Tombstone Street, Metal
Street, Salt Street, Fan Street . . . Today, bamboo
ladders are sold on Sails Street and silk clothes on
Hemp Street. As before, craftspeople still set up next
to one another, offering the same goods as always.
For a while, Maman and I lived on Chicken and
Medicinal Herbs Street in Hanoi. Of the two rows
of *gà tần* restaurants, we preferred the one with
the second-floor patio that wrapped around a big
banyan tree.

ăn hàng

~

street food

WHEN MY HUSBAND fell sick for the first time, I prepared a dish for him that involved gently cooking chicken with lotus seeds, ginkgo nuts and dried goji berries. According to certain beliefs, a portion of eternity stays behind in the lotus, while the ginkgo strengthens the neurons, since its leaves are shaped like brains. As for the goji berries, books attesting to their medicinal virtues have existed since the days of emperors and princesses. The benefits of the dish are likely due to the attention devoted to its preparation. In addition to the long hours of slow cooking, the shell of the ginkgo must be cracked firmly but with restraint, to protect the whole of the tender flesh. And the green germ must be removed from the lotus seeds to get rid of their bitter taste.

It's rare that bitterness is totally eliminated, because it's often found in foods considered to be cold, those that don't inflame us— unlike mangoes, hot peppers, chocolate. It's believed that we should cut back on tastes we enjoy too easily because they're bad for us, while a bitter taste restores the balance. I could have avoided separating the lotus seeds in two to eliminate the germs, which may be drunk in infusions to bring on sleep. But I wanted to avoid extremes: extreme tastes, extreme sensations.

DURING THE THREE DAYS of my husband's fever, I
fed him, a mouthful at a time. In Vietnam, when we
don't know what has caused a death, we blame the
wind, as if catching an impure wind could kill us.
That's why I asked him to take off his shirt so I could
chase away the bad wind by scratching his back with a
porcelain spoon moistened with a few drops of tiger
balm. I had never looked at a man's skin so close up.
I drew his skeleton on it by rubbing between the
bones and the length of his spine. Dark red blotches
emerged on the surface, eliminating the heat and
perhaps all the pains that had never been felt. I
repeated those ancient movements to care for a
stranger who had become my only anchoring point.
I would have liked to know how to comfort him, run
my hand over his skin. All I could do was warm him
with the blanket that still smelled of the long journey
from the Chinese factory to our apartment.

cạo gió

~

scratching
the wind

AS SOON AS HE was able to get back on his feet, he
resumed serving Tonkinese soups to his customers.
Many were bachelors waiting for their Vietnamese
wives or to have the fare needed for plane tickets.
Most came for a bowl of soup three or four times a
week. They would arrive before opening on Saturday
or Sunday morning for a filter coffee with my husband, and compared the length of time they had to
wait with that of the drops of coffee that dripped onto
the condensed milk in their glasses. I served the same
breakfast to everyone, but I changed what was on
offer every morning to the rhythm of my virtual visit
to the streets of Vietnam.

I read once that in Japan each town specializes in
one kind of cake. Men travelling on business often
bring home a box of desserts from the town where
they've been. Sometimes a man doesn't leave the town
where he lives, only his wife, temporarily, to be with
his mistress. The men allow themselves now and then
to withdraw from their real lives, to take a vacation. In
that case, there are shops that, anticipating those sorts
of absences, offer men cakes from different towns.

As in Japan and maybe everywhere else,
Vietnamese towns and villages have their specialties
too. So I only had to go back mentally to Chợ Lớn, the
big Chinese neighbourhood in Saigon, to get the idea
of preparing pork meatballs wrapped around a small
piece of sparerib, steamed in a trickle of tomato sauce.
This dish is unfailingly served with a baguette, as if

France had always been part of Sino-Vietnamese culinary traditions. Week after week, clients who were friends of my husband received their plate or their bowl with ever-greater anticipation.

One of the men came from Rạch Giá, a coastal town where a meal-in-a-bowl—a poached fish with vermicelli, embellished with shrimp eggs and caramelized pork—had been invented. Tears ran down his cheeks when I sprinkled his bowl with a small spoonful of pickled garlic. Eating that soup, he murmured that he had tasted his land, the land where he'd grown up, where he was loved.

On busy weekend mornings, customers who were also friends were content with a bowl of rice covered with an *ốp la* (fried egg) salted with soy sauce. This way they began their day off with a certain feeling of quiet happiness.

WITHIN A FEW MONTHS, those clients who'd come on their own in the beginning began to turn up with a colleague, a neighbour, a woman friend. The more people waiting in the entrance and then outside on the sidewalk, the more nights I spent in the kitchen. Fairly soon, clients stopped ordering *soupe tonkinoise* in favour of the plat du jour, even if they didn't know what was on the menu before they arrived at the restaurant and read the blackboard hanging in the window. Just one dish per day. One memory at a time, because it took me a lot of effort not to let my emotions overflow the plates. And yet every time the salt shaker fell accidentally and covered the floor with white grains, I had to restrain myself from counting them, as Maman always did when her daily ration was limited to thirty grains. Fortunately, the growing number of clients kept me from losing my focus.

VERY SOON, I COULD no longer count the number
of plates to wash. My husband hired a young
Vietnamese man. He came equipped with a high-
volume smile. Before he said a word, we could hear
his good humour burst out in his stomach like pop-
corn. I couldn't help laughing hard, so hard, when
he pulled on the yellow rubber gloves he'd taken
from his pockets, shouting: "Ta-dah!" I didn't think
I could be capable of producing such a reverberating,
spontaneous sound. He quickly became my little
brother, a ray of sunlight that never faded, even
when life presented nearly insurmountable hardships.
Whenever he had a spare moment, he would be
studying. He repeated chemistry formulas, his head
in a fog of steam from the dishwasher. He posted the
periodic table of the elements on the tile wall. He
wrote the definitions of words in the margins of pages
in novels he was reading for his coursework. In spite
of all his efforts, he repeatedly failed his philosophy
and French exams. It was his last chance to pass when
I met him. I spent many nights reading his homework
and correcting his essays.

hồn nhiên

~

spontaneous

lỗi

~

mistakes

AS SOON AS I KNEW how to write, Maman insisted on a dictation every evening, power failure or not. She read to me from Maupassant by the light of an oil lamp the size of a drinking glass. We took turns having the light from the flame. After each sentence, I had to perform a logical, grammatical and syntactical analysis. Before she went to bed, Maman put the book back in its metal box and buried it in its hiding place. It was the biggest secret, because foreign books were prohibited, especially novels and, more specifically, the triviality of fiction.

THANKS TO THAT COACHING, I was able to draft
the ten questions that my sun-brother had been given
by his philosophy teacher. He would have to answer
just one, but he wouldn't know which before the
exam. I wrote ten answers for him, which he learned
by heart, because my explanations in Vietnamese
didn't help him. So this was how he obtained his
diploma and got a job while continuing to give me a
hand on weekends. One night he told me that earlier
that day in his factory, a girl who'd recently been
hired had come and stood close to him. Without
turning towards me, he dropped a big kettle into
the sink to imitate the electric current that had shot
through his body from the top of his head to his feet.
He threw up his arms, hands clad in yellow gloves,
and took root in the ground as if he'd been struck
by lightning. I stood there flabbergasted before his
trance state, thinking he was acting delirious and
crazy. But he was just in love. I didn't know that
condition to be able to identify it, to recognize it.
Still, I was carried away in the wake of his euphoria,
playing Cyrano de Bergerac to help him court that
girl whom I barely knew.

HER NAME WAS BẠCH, she was Vietnamese, she'd arrived a short time before and was sad to leave her village at the southern tip of Vietnam. She lived with an aunt in a Montreal suburb, in a big, dust-free house where every room had its designated slippers and each cutting board a specific use. The aunt had sponsored Bạch and her family of six. She would have preferred to stay in Cà Mau with her friends, embroidering tablecloths for export. Her aunt, though, had persuaded her parents that they must relinquish their life that held no promise, sacrifice their own generation so the next one could be educated. And so Bạch found herself in a factory that made electronic scoreboards. She soldered circuits with ease because her fingers had already been trained to fill space with a needle, stitch by stitch.

My sun-brother started by bringing her whatever I had in the kitchen: slices of manioc cake, fried rice with crab, or chicken with ginger and shiitake mushrooms. He came running to me, shrieking with the intense, immortal happiness of youth, when he managed to escort her back to her aunt's for the first time. Eventually he succeeded in asking for her hand in marriage. I don't know if she agreed because he saved her the four hours of bus trips every day or because she had decided to let herself be loved. But the wedding went ahead.

I VOLUNTEERED TO HELP with the preparations for
the engagement party because my sun-brother's father
worked sixty-hour weeks at a factory that made brake
pads and another ten hours delivering pizzas, while
violent migraines and painkillers reduced his mother
to the state of a drunken reed, constantly disturbed by
drafts. Sometimes the mere breath of a murmur on
her cheek was enough to rattle her and cause the map
of her life's journey to appear on her forehead. It was
unthinkable, then, to use her living room for wrap-
ping the gifts in the traditional translucent red paper
to take to the bride's house, since the sound made by
every fold, every movement, would be enough to slash
open her skin. To spare her the crackling, rustling and
commotion, we chose the restaurant dining room as
headquarters.

ON THE EVE OF THE engagement party, the room was aglow with red—not the red of love but that of luck. Superstition dictated that each gift be wrapped in that colour, which represents good fortune, because all newlyweds need a lot of luck to find the balance that allows two individuals to build a single shared life, one that will support others in turn. We wish them not love but happiness in duplicate: the word is written twice, one linked to the other, mirrored, cloned. Since no one dares take a risk, each tray of gifts, without exception, is covered with bright red cloth, embroidered with the word *happiness*, not plural but doubled.

Luckily, newlyweds don't burden themselves with the worries of those who have lived the ordeal before them. They are just here for the party and they believe that happiness inevitably comes with marriage, or the opposite.

TO CONTRIBUTE TO THE NEXT PART, to the natural cycle of life, my husband had mobilized clients who were friends to form the delegation that would carry the platters of gifts on the morning of the ceremony. The lacquered suckling pig had been entrusted to the strongest, while the others divided up the platter of boxes of tea, bottles of wine and biscuits. The cousins were responsible for the jewels, the small teapot filled with rice alcohol, and the platter of betel leaves and areca nuts. Today, very few Vietnamese still chew areca nuts, but all the same they symbolize the beginning of an encounter. Less than a hundred years ago, the Vietnamese received their guests with a mother-of-pearl wooden box containing a cylindrical mortar for crushing the nut before it was rolled up in a leaf lightly covered with lime. Regular users say the mixture provides the same stimulation as coffee, while those with weak hearts talk about dizzy spells or even intoxication. The effect is achieved by slow chewing, which colours the saliva red—the red of drunkenness, the red of love—because this red tells the story of an eternal union.

According to legend, twin brothers were in love with the same girl. The first married her. The second, choked with sorrow, left the village so his brother wouldn't notice. The broken-hearted brother walked until he was exhausted, until he was transformed into limestone. The other twin took the same road in search of his brother. He dropped dead of fatigue next

trầu cau

~

areca nuts

to the rock and metamorphosed into a betel palm. His wife followed his tracks and in the same place was turned into a climbing vine with heart-shaped leaves, wound around the trunk of the palm tree that shaded the rock. I have often wondered how that love triangle had been able to become the symbol of a happy marriage, because the end proved so sad. I think we misunderstood our ancestors. They placed the platter of betel at the head of the procession because they wanted to warn the newlyweds of the danger of impossible loves, not the opposite. Or did they want to warn us that love can kill?

THOUGH THE COUPLE BOWS LOW, noses to the
ground, the ancestors hanging on the wall above the
altar will never give them the true reason. They will
be content to watch the incense sticks burn and to
observe the transmission of rituals from one generation to the next. They know that one day the mothers-
in-law will no longer offer earrings to their new
daughters-in-law. Already, hardly anyone remembers
that at the engagement party the mothers insert into
the brides' earlobes gold balls that represent buds. At
the marriage, the mothers-in-law replace them with
earrings in the shape of full-blown flowers that
symbolize the blossoming of the bride, her
defloration.

lạytổ tiên
~
bowing to
the ancestors

FROM MY IN-LAWS, all I got was an envelope that must have been worth its weight in gold because the papers in it offered me another elsewhere and an unknown life with a stranger. Since I had neither father nor ancestors, they'd thought it best to avoid ceremony. I left for the airport with no convoys of cousins and friends, unlike the other passengers. There were hundreds outside the airport, children, old people, tears, promises, all tangled up in emotions. In those years, people went away with no hope of returning. They only promised not to forget. Unlike other Vietnamese mothers, who counted on the loyalty and gratitude of their children, Maman wanted me to forget, to forget her because I now had a chance to start again, to go away with no baggage, to reinvent myself. But that was impossible.

WHEN VIETNAMESE PEOPLE MEET, native village
and family tree are the two subjects that open most
conversations, because we firmly believe that we are
what our ancestors have been, that our destinies
respond to what we have done in the lives that came
before us. The oldest knew my grandfather by name
or in person, that man I had never met. The younger
ones remembered Maman's brothers and sisters and
knew that I didn't resemble them. They envied my
slender legs, but they feared the scandalous story
hinted at by my overly pronounced curves. Only those
Québécois clients who had adopted a child in Vietnam
dared to approach me with a neutral gaze, to offer me
a blank page.

gia đình

~

family

JULIE WAS THE FIRST to stick her head into the opening through which I delivered the plates. Her smile stretched from one side of the aperture to the other. The enthusiasm of her greeting was like that of an archaeologist upon discovering a trace of the first kiss. Promptly, before even a word was uttered, we became friends and, with time, sisters. She adopted me as she'd adopted her daughter, without questioning our past. She took me to see movies in the afternoon, or we would watch classics at her place. She opened her refrigerator and had me taste its contents in no particular order, according to her mood of the day: from smoked meat to tourtière, ketchup to *sauce béchamel*, and including celery root, rhubarb, bison, *pouding chômeur* and pickled eggs. Sometimes Julie would come and cook with me. I would show her how to keep sticky rice in superimposed layers of banana leaves by squeezing them firmly but without smothering the rice. It's always a fragile balance, one that fingers can feel better than words can explain.

At the end of every January, we had to prepare several dozen of the treats because my husband wanted to offer them to his friends and his distant relatives for the Vietnamese New Year, as his mother used to do in her village. The scent of banana leaves cooked in boiling water for many hours reminded him of the days before Tết when the whole neighbourhood spent the night feeding the fire under cauldrons full of rice rolls stuffed with mung bean paste, smooth and as discreetly yellow as the moon.

Julie came to our restaurant often. She invited her friends for lunch, organized monthly meetings of her book group, and reserved the entire restaurant to celebrate family birthdays and wedding anniversaries. Every time, she brought me out of the kitchen to be introduced to her guests, embracing me with her whole body. She was the big sister I'd never had, and I was her daughter's Vietnamese mother.

ONE NIGHT, SHE PLACED a key on my kitchen counter while I was using tweezers to remove the minute impurities in the fine filaments of a swallow's nest, making sure it was perfect without wasting a single drop of the soup. My husband had bought that precious find, which was traded for thousands of dollars a kilo, from a vendor of medicinal and Chinese herbs. He maintained that the swallows showed a patient and infinite love for their fledglings because they were the only birds that built their nests using only their saliva. And so to eat those nests would give us a better chance of becoming parents in turn. I didn't have time to explain to Julie how rare that potion was because she insisted on dragging me towards the exit and had me put the key in the lock next door. And so our adventure began.

JULIE HAD BROUGHT ARCHITECTS and decorators
to turn the space into a culinary workshop. She had
asked her husband, who often travelled to Asia on
business, to look for a used bicycle-powered rickshaw
in Vietnam, and he'd sent her one whose metal
structure was partly rusted and whose saddle was
bent out of shape by sweat. On the wall, she had
mounted two long wooden panels engraved with
two lines of Chinese characters that echoed each
other, as was done at the entrance to old mandarin
residences. She had ordered from Huế some conical
hats adorned with poems inserted between the
braided latania leaves and sixteen bamboo circles
to be offered as gifts at the opening. At the back of the
restaurant, she'd built a large bookcase. Cookbooks
and photos were arranged on the shelves, standing
at attention, obedient and upright as the children in
the schoolyard who sang the national anthem every
morning in front of the apartment where Maman and
I had lived. Julie held my hand and walked me along
the wall, preventing me from falling to my knees
when I saw the last shelf, where she'd placed a row
of novels of which I'd only ever read a page or two
or sometimes a chapter, but never the whole book.

A great many books in French or English had been
confiscated during the years of political chaos. We
would never know the fate of those books, but some
did survive, in pieces. We would never know what
road whole pages had travelled, only to end up in the

xích lô

~

rickshaw

hands of merchants who used them to wrap bread, a catfish or a bunch of water spinach. No one could ever tell me why I'd been so lucky as to turn up those treasures buried under piles of yellowing newspapers. Maman told me that the pages were forbidden fruits fallen from heaven.

From these precious harvests, I had remembered the word *lassitude* from *Bonjour tristesse*, by Françoise Sagan; *langueur* from Verlaine; and *pénitentiaire* from Kafka. Maman had also explained the meaning of fiction with this sentence by Albert Camus in *L'Étranger*, for it was unthinkable to us that a woman could show desire: "In the evening, Marie came looking for me and asked if I wanted to marry her." And then there was Marius; without knowing the beginning or the end of his story in *Les Misérables*, to me he was a hero because one time our monthly ration of a hundred grams of pork had been draped in these words: "Life, hardship, isolation, poverty, are battlefields that have their heroes: obscure heroes sometimes greater than the illustrious ones."

THERE WERE MANY WORDS whose meaning   *tự điển*
Maman didn't know. Luckily, we had ready access to   ~
a living dictionary. He was older than Maman. The   dictionary
neighbours thought he was crazy because every day
he stood under the rose apple tree, where he recited
words in French and their definitions. His dictionary,
which he had held close to him throughout his
childhood, had been confiscated, but he went on
turning the pages in his head. I just had to say a word
to him through the fence that separated us and he
would give me the definition. And one time, he had
given me the rosiest of the rose apples from the bunch
that hung just above his head when I gave him the
verb *to sniff.*

"Sniff: to breathe in through the nose in order to
smell. To sniff the air. The wind. The fog. To sniff
the fruit! Sniff! Rose apple, in Guyana known also as
love apple. Sniff!"

After that lesson, I never ate a love apple without
first sniffing the glossy, fuchsia-pink skin, its innocent
coolness nearly hypnotic. And it's why I quite naturally
chose that fruit out of the dozens of other exotic fruits
made of plaster that Julie had arranged on a big plate in
the middle of the reading table. I brought it to my nose
and its sweetly fresh perfume seized me as if its white
flesh were tender and real. Julie burst out laughing. "If
you want to smell something real, come here."

She opened the glass door of a big cupboard
holding dozens of small glass bottles filled with spices:

star anise, cloves, turmeric, coriander seeds, powdered galangal . . . The inevitable bottles of fish sauce were there too, along with vermicelli and rice wrappers.

For months, Julie toiled in the workshop non-stop, but also with me, on me. She persuaded me to organize a series of Vietnamese cooking lessons and tastings. I went along with her because her enthusiasm was irresistible.

LIFE WAS COMING AT ME like a canvas Julie was
unrolling before my eyes. New colours, new shapes
revealed themselves as I progressed, as the roll was
unwound. And as if by enchantment, images
appeared that sketched a scene or illustrated a
moment. Suddenly, the painter's movements became
audible and palpable. In the same way, a voice
emerged from my name—*mān*—written in jade
green on the plates, on bags, on the front window.
The first group of twenty who came to the workshop
amplified that budding voice as they took home
recipes and repeated stories told around the table.
The vibrant life of that adventure launched another
life, the one that had finally come and settled in the
warmth of my belly.

tranh

~

painting

JULIE AND MY HUSBAND combined efforts to find me permanent kitchen help. Hồng was scarcely older than me but already had a teenage daughter. She had met her Québécois husband in a Saigon café; she was a waitress, he was a client. He had shown her his Canadian passport and she had agreed to the journey so that her daughter could stop smelling tobacco smoke and feeling the sweat of strangers' hands on her smock when she came home from work in the middle of the night. He was in love with Hồng, in love with his time in Vietnam, where his hundred dollars were worth a million dongs, where a thousand dollars let him live the experience of eternal love. He had long dreamed of her when he went back to his apartment full of empty bottles.

Had she known Andy Warhol, Hồng would have appreciated the walls plastered with rows and rows of beer bottles like a piece of pop art. Unfortunately, all she saw was the entrance to a dark tunnel. She disappointed him by choosing skirts that were too long and shoes that were too flat, and he criticized her for leaving too early and coming home from the factory too late. Hồng was surprised to find out that the apartment didn't belong to him and that his car coughed like an old man in the rain. But she was grateful for the bed for her daughter, so she rolled up her sleeves to erase the marks of her husband's loneliness and to allow light into the narrow hallways, whose walls had absorbed the shock of closed fists and silenced fury.

HỒNG WORKED DAY AND NIGHT, weekdays and weekends. She hoped that her husband would do the same, that he would look for more clients, that he would cut the lawns of more houses. There were days, though, when the sky was so heavy it was impossible for him to get up. That was how she met Julie, because Hồng had replaced her husband behind the lawn mower once, twice, several times. The last time, Julie had come outside, offered her a glass of water and suggested to my husband that she could help me out in the restaurant.

cỏ

~

lawn

AT FIRST, HÔNG KEPT her distance. I only heard
her moving around, efficient, extraordinary. Thanks
to her, I was able to leave the kitchen and go to New
York with Julie and spend two whole afternoons in a
gigantic bookstore where hundreds of cookbooks
opened in front of us. We had very little time, so Julie
took me to one restaurant for an appetizer, to a second
one for the meal, and to yet another for dessert. She
wanted me to visit as many addresses as possible in
forty-eight hours. Julie knew Manhattan and its
warehouses, which held paintings and sculptures that
made me dizzy. How had Richard Serra imagined
that rust-covered steel was sensual? How does a
person transport a work of art twenty times bigger
than my kitchen? How does a person think so big?

JULIE SHOWED ME SOMETHING outside my everyday life to make me see the horizon, so that I would desire the horizon. She wanted me to learn to breathe deeply, no longer just sufficiently. A hundred times, she repeated the same message, in a hundred variations:

"Bite. Bite into the apple."

"Bite the way the file bites metal."

"Bite hard and make the most of life."

"Bite! Bite! Bite!" she said, laughing hard, as she pulled my hand to cross the street or while she was braiding my hair. She educated me in languages, in gestures, in emotions. Julie talked as much with her hands as with her wrinkled nose, while I could barely maintain her gaze for the duration of a sentence. Several times, she stood me in front of a mirror, obliging me to talk with her while we looked at ourselves, so that I could observe the stillness of my body compared with hers.

I was floored every time Julie repeated words in Vietnamese. She imitated accents with the flexibility of a gymnast and the precision of a musician. She pronounced the five versions of *la, là, lạ, lả, lã*, distinguishing the tones even if she didn't understand the different definitions: to cry, to be, stranger, to faint, cool. The challenge I'd devised was much too easy for her, while the exercise she'd suggested in turn required an enormous effort from me. Learning songs by heart was not a demanding task in itself, but

căn

~

bite

singing them out loud took all my courage. Julie made the sounds come out by loosening my tongue.

"Stick out your tongue. Try to touch your chin. Turn towards the left . . . now, towards the right. And again."

She roared with laughter at the sight of me putting my hand a few centimetres from my mouth during those exercises, making me giggle every time. Julie's laugh was tremendously warm, tremendously charming, but she would also shed abundant tears, unlike Vietnamese women, who cry as silently as possible. Only professional mourners hired for funerals could gesticulate and display pain on their features without being considered inelegant.

MY HUSBAND NEVER KNEW that on the nights I wrote to Maman, I cried. Or if he did know, he preferred to console me by always having booklets of stamps in the drawer. Maman didn't reply very often. Maybe because she didn't want to cry either. I heard the echo of her silence, though, and the burden of everything that couldn't be heard. At night, when we used to share the same bed, the sound of Maman's tears sometimes escaped the corners of her closed eyes. I would hold my breath then, because with no witness, sorrow might exist only as a ghost.

Most Vietnamese believe in the existence of wandering souls who haunt life, who watch for death, who stay wedged between the two. Every year, in the seventh lunar month, people burn incense, paper money and garments to help the ghosts to free themselves, to leave the world of the living, which has not anticipated a place for them. When I threw the false paper money, orange and gold, into the fire, I hoped for both the ghosts and Maman's sadness to disappear, even if she denied the ghosts' existence with the same fervour as the Communist Party, which condemned the people's fear of those roving spirits, unidentifiable and with no witnesses.

It's true that Maman's face, like my husband's, showed neither pain nor joy, to say nothing of pleasure, while I could read everything on Julie's. When she wept, full of affection, at the birth of my son, her heart was drawn on her cheeks, her forehead, her lips. In the same way, she was moved when she carried children just arrived from faraway lands to greet their new destiny in the cocoons carefully woven for them in Montreal. She took their photos and gave them greeting cards signed by her friends in the adoptive parents' group. She was the first to say, "I love you," to my baby who was still curled up in my belly. She was also the one who took my husband's hand to place it against the little foot that was imprinted on my stretched skin. Then, despite his stiff body language, she was quite ready to take him in her arms when he agreed to sponsor Maman for her immigration to Canada.

IT TOOK SEVERAL YEARS and countless photos of
my two children to persuade Maman to join me.
Unlike my boy, my little girl arrived very quickly, at
the same speed as the multiplication of catering orders
for private and corporate parties. My husband had
bought the duplex next door to enlarge our living
space. At the same time, Julie was building a large
kitchen under the workshop and she turned the two
apartments above us into a daycare for her daughter,
my children, and now and then the children of friends
who found themselves without a sitter. Two ladies
from the Philippines took turns helping out during
parties that ended too late or mornings that started
before dawn.

In the kitchen, Julie had hired Philippe, a pastry
chef, to reinvent Vietnamese desserts, because our
traditions regarding cream, chocolate and cakes were
limited to a few, very basic recipes. As a matter of
fact, Vietnamese call birthday cakes *bánh gatô*, with
bánh meaning "bread-cake-batter." We had to import
the word *gatô* because cake comes from a singular
culinary tradition. We had to learn how to use butter,
milk, vanilla, chocolate—ingredients that were as
foreign to us as the cooking methods. Lacking ovens,
Vietnamese women baked their cakes in a cauldron
covered with a lid on which they placed chunks of
blazing coal. The cauldron was set on a terracotta
barbecue the size of an average cachepot so the
mixture could be elevated and baked without

burning even if the temperature couldn't be constant or the heat distribution uniform. I was very surprised, then, at Philippe's thermometer as well as his stopwatch and his set of measuring spoons, not to mention implements as mysterious as they were impressive. I ran my hand over the contents of the drawers and shelves with the fascination of a child stepping into a cockpit.

Slowly, Philippe brought me into his world. He started with hazelnuts, plain, roasted, whole, ground—because I adore nuts. From Chinatown, I would bring him pandan leaves to share with him their intensely green colour and their scent: in Thailand, taxi drivers place a fresh bouquet under their seat every two or three days. As Philippe was already familiar with lychees, I offered him their cousins, longans, whose glossy seeds often serve as a metaphor for a pretty girl's eyes, and rambutans, with their red peel and hairy surface like a sea urchin, but soft to the touch.

My Vietnamese-style banana cake was delicious, but it looked frightening, sturdy and uncouth as it was. In no time, Philippe softened it with foamy caramel made from raw cane sugar. Thus he married East and West, as with the cake with whole bananas fitted into baguette dough soaked in coconut milk and cow's milk. Five hours' baking at a low temperature forced the bread to play a protective role for the fruit as the bananas slowly delivered up the sugar in their flesh. Anyone lucky enough to taste that cake freshly baked could see, when cutting it, the crimson of the bananas embarrassed at being caught in the act.

PHILIPPE ENHANCED AND ENNOBLED the desserts
that the Vietnamese call simply by the number of
colours in the ingredients: *chè* three colours, *chè* five
colours, *chè* seven colours. Each merchant has her
own interpretation of the dessert, which is usually
eaten as a snack on the sidewalk at a corner, sitting on
a small stool when school lets out, or between two
destinations with friends. I think that meeting
someone for *chè* usually means a date in a café, except
that there it's made with blends of mung bean paste,
tapioca in the shape of pomegranate seeds, red beans,
black-eyed peas or the fruit of the nipa palm, all
topped with a mountain of crushed ice. A good many
secrets were shared between two spoonfuls of *chè* and
a good many love affairs were born in that place,
which often had no address.

In our workshop, when they tasted Philippe's
creations, the clients' confidences scented the air, and
sometimes they kissed passionately as if they were
alone, set back from time. I had never seen people so
much in love so close up before. Nor had I ever heard
"I love you" spoken aloud, as Julie did every day.
She never hung up the phone without saying "I love
you" to her husband and her daughter. I sometimes
tried to put into words my gratitude towards Julie,
but I was never really successful. I could only show
my affection through everyday acts, such as preparing
for her, during her numerous appointments and
before she even felt the urge, the lime soda she

adored, or by unplugging the phones in her office when I made her take a fifteen-minute nap, or by rubbing a turmeric root on a freshly healed sore to prevent it from scarring. I thanked heaven when I had the chance to look after her daughter for five, seven or ten days so she could join her husband in Turkey, Japan or Sri Lanka. I could offer her only my friendship, because Julie lacked nothing, she had so much to give and she gave everything to everyone. She was a merchant of happiness.

THEY SAY THAT HAPPINESS cannot be bought.
What I learned from Julie is that on its own, happiness multiplies, is shared, and adapts to each of us. It
was within that happiness that the years accumulated
one after another, paying no attention to calendar or
seasons. I could not say at what moment exactly Hồng
took the helm of the restaurant kitchen. I only know
that, very early one morning, I opened my eyes and
saw a world so perfect it made me dizzy. Beside me,
my husband's face was pressed into the pillow, rested,
peaceful, and wrapped in a nearly palpable film of
calm and stillness. In the adjacent rooms, my children
were fast asleep. I had the impression I could hear
their dreams, where even the monsters seem playful
or are transformed into gentlemen. Maman had
chosen her domain at the end of the corridor joining
the two apartments. She involved herself in the
children's homework as rigorously as a substitute
teacher. I often caught her smiling discreetly when
they called her *Bà Ngoại*, maternal grandmother.
During school hours, she insisted on helping Hồng in
the kitchen and refused to join the Vietnamese
community seniors' club.

And so Maman injected new life into our restaurant by adding recipes to our menu now and then,
which continued to follow only our regular customers' wishes and the happenstance of our memories.

HÔNG AND HER DAUGHTER became members of the family when they moved into the apartment that had been used as the children's daycare. She had left her husband when Julie caught a glimpse of the bruises scattered over her body. Hidden by long sleeves and dark trousers, it was possible to forget them. The *bravo*s and the *thank you*s of the customers also erased the unwitting abuse and the oblivious insults that alcohol poured onto her. She pushed forward head-long, ignoring her nights, disregarding blows, using her body as a shield to protect her daughter from the threat of being sent back to Vietnam, where she thought she would no longer fit in. It was easy to close her eyes because the only two mirrors in the dark apartment reflected more the explosion of anger than her silhouette, which appeared there in fragments. She had forgotten what she looked like in one piece until the day she saw herself in Julie's eyes when she accidentally opened the bathroom door as Hông was taking off her chef's jacket.

We went in a four-car convoy, two women and six men, to rescue Hông and her daughter from a reality that had become a way of life, a habit. Her husband never put to the test the army that stood upright behind her that night and every night thereafter. Before we had time to sort through photos and arrange them in albums, Hông's daughter had started her first year in medicine at university and we were launching the first cookbook from our atelier-boutique-restaurant.

hông

~

pink and
sometimes red

THE LAUNCH WAS GIVEN a lot of media coverage thanks to our faithful and enthusiastic admirers, and above all thanks to Julie's network, which included radio and TV as well as print. A successful broadcast would generate a flattering review. Before the first newspaper article had been framed, magazines filled our precious rigid suitcase made of leather and wood that seemed to have crossed the Indian Ocean, trod the Silk Road or survived the Holocaust. It was set on a folding stand in the window, wide open, rich with all the praise that might come from as far away as the United States and France. In the *Weekend à Montréal* guide, our atelier-restaurant Mān was among the essential addresses, while for Frommer's it was an experience not to be missed. Quebeckers' interest in Vietnamese cuisine was growing along with the increased opening of Vietnam's doors to mass tourism. That wave of enthusiasm turned our business into a home base, our book *La Palanche* (The Yoke) into a cultural reference and me into a spokesperson. Readers praised the recipes but often wanted to talk to me about the tales and anecdotes that had inspired our choices.

The story of the little nine-year-old girl imprisoned for several months after trying to escape by boat explained the taste of tomato and parsley soup better than the picture next to the recipe. We had chosen it in honour of Hồng. She was that little girl, separated from her father and her older brother

during their arrest. Minutes before her father pushed
her into the crowd crammed onto the boat, he had
told her that in no circumstances was she to identify
him. She had to tell the police she was travelling
alone with her twelve-year-old brother. She'd ended
up in the women's prison, isolated from the men's by
sheets of metal. Her brother had dug a small space
under it so he could hold her hand during the night.
In daytime she would go all the way to the end of
the camp, where only a wire fence separated them.
That way, her brother could keep an eye on her.
Their father kept as far from his children as possible,
changing his name and lying about his address. He
never turned around, even when he heard them,
sitting on their heels on soil dried by the pacing
prisoners, crying from fear and hunger. He hoped
that their innocence and their loneliness would allow
them to be freed before him. His wish was granted.
The children went back to the house, whereas he
remained, even after the prison had been shut down
for years.

Hồng's final memory of her father is a faded
yellow plastic bowl filled with clear broth and a piece
of tomato and a few bits of parsley stem. He had
placed it in a corner of the yard, going past her
brother, who had held on to the bowl in the circle of
his folded legs and waited for Hồng to arrive at the
fence to make her drink a little of the tomato water.
She had never tasted anything so delicious. Since her

liberation, she had been trying to re-create those tastes by making the soup at least once a week. No matter what variety of tomato she tried, she never managed to reproduce the indelible but elusive memory of those few sips. And so we immortalized the recipe in memory of her father.

LA PALANCHE WAS A resounding success across the
province, so much so that a producer suggested a
television cooking show. I wanted to broaden the
experiment we'd worked on with Philippe, so Julie
invited chefs to revisit or to reinvent our Vietnamese
recipes on screen, with me. These collaborations
confirmed for us that mainly we were creating the
same balance of tastes in the mouth but by using
ingredients specific to each chef's region. The osso
bucco was brightened up by gremolata, while the
lemongrass beef stew was served with pickled daikon
for its slightly bitter taste. In traditional Québécois
cuisine, beef meatballs are cooked in a brown sauce
whose consistency and colour resembles the one based
on soya and fermented black beans that garnishes
grilled Vietnamese meatballs. In Louisiana, fish is
coated in Cajun spices to blacken it, while the
Vietnamese use lemongrass and minced garlic.

Of course, certain tastes have an exclusive identity
and well-defined borders. For instance, none of the
chefs I met knew what to do with the cartilage in
chicken bones, while people in Bangkok go into
ecstasies over those breaded lumps. It would be cruel
of me to impose fermented shrimp paste, intensely
mauve and aromatic, on my guest chefs, as it would be
to feed them green guavas drenched in salt with very
hot peppers. Salmon, however, grilled or fried, goes
well with a salad of green mango and ginger. Like
friends of long standing, fish sauce goes perfectly with

maple syrup in a marinade for spareribs, while in a soup made with tamarind, tomatoes, pineapple and fish, celery is a worthy substitute for the stems of elephant ears. The two vegetables absorb the flavours and carry the broth into their porous flesh as submissively as a servant, at the same time as present as an aspirate *h*. Oddly enough, the leaf of the elephant ear, unlike its porous stem, could provide shelter from rain because it is impermeable, like the leaves of water lilies and lotus blossoms. Julie, charmed by the two facets of those plants, had a pond dug in the restaurant's backyard for floating tropical flowers. As soon as the first bud appeared, Maman would recite a popular traditional song that every Vietnamese knows by heart:

Trong đầm gì đẹp bằng sen,
Lá xanh, bông trắng lại chen nhụy vàng,
Nhụy vàng, bông trắng, lá xanh,
Gần bùn mà chẳng hôi tanh mùi bùn.

What is lovelier than the lotus in the swamp,
Its green leaves compete with white petals, with
    yellow pistils,
Yellow pistils, white petals, green leaves,
Near to the mud but without its stench.

WE PRINTED HUNDREDS OF copies of both versions
of this poem to offer to our customers, who came to
bask in the garden on canvas beach chairs. Students,
often aspiring writers or poets, would meet on the
patio under Maman's giant squash plants, to write
side by side, exchange one word for another, and
reassure those who panicked over the blank page.
Unobtrusively, in the privacy of that urban oasis,
books were launched and texts regularly read by their
authors on nights when the moon was full.

AT THE SAME TIME, *La Palanche* was winning
over Paris, where many readers had a close relationship with Vietnam. For some it called to mind a
grandfather who'd lived there at the time of French
Indochina, others remembered an uncle or a distant
cousin describing the plantations of "the wood that
weeps," the rubber tree that bled latex by the ton.
Vietnamese revolutionaries had shattered the roman-
tic image of hectares covered with lines of those tall,
upright trees by lifting the curtain of mist that hid the
sweat and the lowered heads of the coolies.

In the pale blue eyes of Francine, a reader I met at
the Paris Salon du Livre, no architecture could
compare with that of the Grall Hospital in Saigon,
where her father, like a demigod, crossed the broad
verandas that surrounded the patients' rooms. He'd
been the chief surgeon there but never had a chance to
go back before he died. In spite of everything,
Vietnam was in his heart until his final breath,
because it was there he had abandoned the wet nurse
who'd brought Francine up for eight years and the
handicapped children from the orphanage he'd built
like a nest, like a challenge to fate. He had battled
human tragedy by making children believe that Santa
Claus existed and that he was so eager to give them
their presents, he'd forgotten to exchange his velvet
outfit for something more tropical.

Francine had grown up among them, an older
sister to the youngest and a little sister to the bigger

ones. She helped feed the small children, patiently holding spoonfuls of rice, and others had taught her how to count on the Chinese abacus. At nap time, her mother played the piano to lull them to sleep. In return, the orphanage staff sang traditional nursery rhymes to put Francine's little brother, Luc, to sleep while their mother baked cakes to celebrate Twelfth Night or the arrival of a child. When the South lost the war against the North and tanks entered the city, Francine's family had boarded the last plane leaving Saigon, with no time to drop by the orphanage. After that, no one could come to terms with the hasty, forced departure except Luc, who was only thirteen months old at the time and did not remember that in the past he also answered to the name Lực, the "strong and all-powerful" little man in his Vietnamese circles.

FRANCINE WAITED UNTIL the Salon closed to
invite me to Luc's restaurant. The address was one of
those mythic places that have come through history,
including the Second World War, when floors were
painted black to conceal the mosaics from the eyes of
Nazi soldiers. Saigon too had survived various
cataclysms, human nature's specialty. I confirmed to
her that the city had changed a lot, that some streets
even had new names. The former rue Catinat, with
its luxury boutiques, had become Đồng Khởi
(Revolutionary Movement), and the Café Givral,
where thin slices of cantaloupe were sold for high
prices, had been demolished to make room for a
modern building with coloured neon lights and
multi-level parking.

However, I also reassured her: the Hôtel Caravelle
had kept its name, the Notre-Dame church still stood
out in the heart of downtown Saigon—motorcycles
drove around it at every hour and at insane speeds—
and she would recognize the many roundabouts,
including the one at the Bến Thành Market. I made a
basic map of the fifteen hundred stands overloaded
with candied fruits, shoes, dried octopus, fresh
vermicelli, rows of fabric. Just as in her memory,
merchants still defend every square centimetre
available in the narrow, bustling aisles, deafening but
so alive. The two of us were immersed in nostalgia, so
enamoured of our own memories of the place that
Luc's arrival at the table made us jump.

"I've read your book," he told me, holding my hand for too long.

THE MISTAKE FOLLOWED FROM that second-too-long when my fingerprints had time to become imbued with his. Could I have done otherwise? I had the hand of a child and his was a man's, with a pianist's fingers, long and enveloping, whose grip commands and reassures. If my jaw had not been locked and my arms linked, I might have quoted these lines by Rumi that had suddenly appeared in my head:

A fine hanging apple
in love with your stone,
the perfect throw that clips my stem.

Julie had chosen those lines for the invitation to an orchard picnic with her circle of adoptive parents. I'd copied the words onto ivory paper thirty times or so, dipping my pen in an inkwell as I'd done when I was little. I searched for a long time before I found the mauve of my childhood, the mauve of every Vietnamese student during the best years of our lives. In hard times, we would write the first draft in pencil, the second in ink, in order to reuse the notebook. We were graded as much on form as on content, because calligraphy translated idea and intention as well as respect. All those years of training when I had a mauve ink stain on my fingers had left me with fine and steady handwriting that I like to use now and then so I won't lose flexibility in the downstrokes and lightness in the upstrokes. So I memorized those words and the precise image of the apple that has come away from the branch at the shock of a stone against the stem. The blotter that absorbed excess ink sometimes depicted, accidentally, the shape of the apple or the apple tree but never that of the stone or the throw. I was far, then, from imagining that one day I would feel like that apple caught up by a hand in the middle of its fall.

I DIDN'T SLEEP AT ALL that night because, on the ceiling, a film of the minutes I'd spent in Luc's presence ran over and over in a loop, sequence by sequence, each shot frozen in a still. I needed to know exactly what had sucked me in and projected me into that state of weightlessness. In my mind I re-examined each of the tessera in the Briare enamels that decorated the bar with a lush landscape, where morning glories were entangled with climbing roses. Was it the naive pink plumage of the cockatoos in the midst of the leaves in the mosaic that had intoxicated me? Or was it the shininess of the copper pan the server was using to prepare the crepe Suzette that had dazzled me? Or the jade green of Luc's eyes?

Colours, like numbers, come to me first in Vietnamese. Moreover, we are not in the habit of distinguishing people by the shade of their hair or the colour of their eyes since Asians have just one tone: from very dark brown to ebony. So I had to keep revisiting the image of his face in close-up to identify the exact colour of his eyes, because blue and green are designated by one word in my mind: *xanh*. His *xanh* represented not blue, then, but green, the green of the waters of Hạ Long Bay or a dark and aged jade green, that of bracelets women wore for decades. It was said that the tones of jade become more intense with the years, that the tender pistachio green grows deeper until it is the shade of a young olive or even an avocado, if the skin of the wrist can give it a patina.

The closer the tints are to lichen, fir, bottle green, the greater the value of the bracelet. At times, then, the mistress of the house would ask the maid to help her age the bracelets by wearing them on her arms. The fragile appearance of jade forces movements to slow down, imposing elegance on gestures even when the hands are chapped or darkened by coal.

Probably that is why Maman put a jade bracelet on me when I was still very young. At the time, I didn't need to soap my hand or to squeeze my palm as do most women who choose to wear the stone, which some people claim is more precious than diamonds. Today, it surrounds my wrist without slipping because the bone has grown to fill the entire rigid circle. Barring some exceptional circumstance, that bracelet will follow me to my final destination. In the meantime, it is my *aide-mémoire* because it doesn't absorb the heat of flames and is never scratched. It reminds me to be solid and, above all, smooth.

I HELD THE BRACELET tightly like a lifeline during
my sleepless night, because I was dizzy at having
accepted Luc's invitation to see him the next day
and also to hear him play clarinet that same evening,
without hesitation, without Francine, without fear.
I followed his voice just as my grandfather had
followed the traces of my grandmother, two people
who had never known me.

Maman told me that this father, who sounded
strict, had asked to be buried with a ceramic jar that
he kept with great care in his cupboard. It contained
some earth he'd taken from the footsteps of his wife
the first time he'd seen her. He had used a leaf of a
plane tree to take the entire print in one go. His
hands were shaking because he had come close to
never finding her. A soccer match that had gone
overtime made him miss the first appointment,
arranged by the matchmaker. He had arrived an hour
late to a closed door and some deeply offended
people. He had left with no regrets, until the moment
when he saw my grandmother's conical hat cross the
barnyard. It was a hat like any other, the kind worn
indiscriminately by women and men of all ages: ivory,
slightly worn, the summit pointing skyward. Yet the
strip of cloth on hers, which went under her chin to
keep it in place, had ties that hung down on either
side. These strips seemed to react differently to the
wind, which rendered the hat remarkable and her,
his future wife, unique.

In my case, it was Luc's hand straightening
Francine's collar over her scarf when he came to say
hello. It was his twisted face on stage and his bursts of
laughter with his musician friends in the light of bare
bulbs. Or maybe it was nothing in particular.

LUC HAD CLIMBED the four floors two steps at a time and arrived at my door instead of being announced by the hotel's reception desk. That morning, he had texted me: "Do you know the word *apprehension*?" I didn't know the meaning of the word and didn't know that I was already inhabiting it.

There are words whose meaning I try to deduce from how they sound, like *colossal*, *disconnect*, *apostil*, others by texture, smell, shape. To grasp the nuances between two related words, to distinguish melancholy from grief, for example, I weigh each one. When I hold them in my hands, one seems to hang like grey smoke while the other is compressed into a ball of steel. I guess and I grope and the answer is as often the right one as the wrong. I constantly make mistakes, and until now the most surprising had to do with the French word *rebelle*, which I thought was a derivative of *belle*: to be *belle* again, because beauty is acquired and then lost. Maman often told me that in case of conflict, it's better to hold back than to insult someone, even if that person is the one at fault. If we taint the other, we soil our mouth, because we must first fill it with anger, blood, venom. Starting then, we are no longer beautiful. I thought that the *re* in the word *rebelle* opened the possibility of a redemption, the one that would let us regain our beauty from before.

I was often wrong, so that time I dared not guess the meaning of the word *apprehension*. I only felt fear when I opened the door to my room.

HE STOOD IN THE hotel corridor for several breaths before he knocked. In one hand he was holding a coat and in the other, two helmets. Still today I try to remember his first words, in vain; at that precise moment, I was probably somewhere else, maybe on the moon. Vietnamese mothers tell children that a woodcutter lives there, sitting under a banyan tree, playing a flute to entertain the moon fairy. Chinese women show the shadows that form the silhouette of a rabbit preparing the recipe for immortality; Japanese women sew for their daughters *hagoromo*, feathered robes like those worn by the fairy who has departed the Earth for the Moon, leaving behind her a besotted emperor. He asked his army to take him to the summit of the highest mountain so that he could be closer to her.

Luc took me into those fairy tales by covering me with his down coat, its sleeves coming down to my knees. "I beg you, please don't protest," he said, bending down to do up the zipper. I locked the door behind us with the vertigo of an astronaut. I'd read that they sometimes suffer from vertigo in space because they lose the notion of up and down. Worse than that, I had also lost left and right.

I CLIMBED AWKWARDLY ONTO the scooter behind him and we drove across Paris to his mother's residence. She wasn't expecting us. She no longer expected anyone. She didn't sing now and didn't care about the person she saw in the mirror. I wondered if she was approaching the state of nirvana, where the soul quietly leaves the body, free of all desire, insensitive to all suffering. Just as Luc was asking me if I was frightened, she placed her hand on my head and started to stroke my hair, slowly, constantly. All around, the walls were covered with photos, including one of her in a bright red T-shirt with a royal blue heart on the chest, sitting at the piano with, in the background, dozing children temporarily freed of their lame bodies.

HER HANDS WERE WEAK NOW, but they still
expressed so much gentleness, perhaps because her
gnarled fingers had written hundreds of letters to her
orphans, never discouraged though she had yet to
receive a reply. All through his childhood, Luc had
to share his mother with those ghosts that haunted
her. At first, she stopped every Vietnamese woman
she ran into on the streets of Paris to ask if she knew
the orphanage. If by misfortune the person had lived
in the same district, she would be invited over and
asked a thousand questions. One day, a lady had told
her that the house had been confiscated and redis-
tributed to five families. The children had been
chased away when the property was first being
divided. Before the lady could describe the silence
that reigned in the neighbourhood during the
operation, Luc's mother had stood up from the table.
As of that day, she had refused to speak to any
Vietnamese, for fear of encountering another one
who would confirm the dark destiny of the children.
She had also kept Francine and Luc away from
possible contact with them.

mồ côi

~

orphan

FRANCINE CAME TO ME excitedly, like a little girl disobeying an outmoded and emotionally restrictive prohibition unjustly imposed by her mother. The week before we first met, in the window of her local bookstore, the cover photo of *La Palanche*—a terracotta bowl half sunk in embers and containing a caramelized fish steak—had moved her to tears. The aroma of fish sauce had struck her as if she were still standing in the kitchenette of the orphanage just as the cook was pouring some into the piping hot mixture of sugar, onion and garlic. That same day, Francine had given the book to Luc. Like her, he had smelled immediately that violent and inimitable aroma that their mother preferred to any other. She fixed that dish at least once a month, with blanched cabbage or sliced cucumbers and steamed rice. As soon as he was able, Luc escaped from the house when *cá kho tộ* was being prepared. He didn't know which he hated more, the smell of cooked *nước mắm* or the atmosphere surrounding this dish that was so heavy with obsession and dependence.

"Would you agree to cook for my mother?"

ON THE WAY HOME, Luc pointed to the poppies
that coloured the edges of the highways. How could
such a fragile flower inch its way through the wild
grasses, defying concrete and asphalt? He explained to
me that their appearance was deceptive, that poppies
could sweep through uncultivated lands or attack a
whole wheat field. A number of painters had been
captivated by their cockscomb colour, but for Luc the
poppy brought to mind Morpheus, who uses the
flower as a magic wand. He just has to touch us gently
with some petals for us to fall asleep and dream sweet
dreams. As for me, I was living a waking dream
where I dared not blink for fear it would all disappear. I discovered Monet's *Coquelicots* at the Musée
d'Orsay, and also the triangle of skin beneath my chin
where Luc's fingers had brushed against me to fasten
and unfasten the buckle of the motorcycle helmet.

THE NEXT DAY, between two appointments for him and between two commitments for me, we went to the thirteenth arrondissement to go shopping with his children, who had the day off school. We zigzagged down the narrow lanes, amid baskets and boxes piled according to some obscure logic known only to the store. The children weren't the least bit intimidated by the size of the crowd or by the din of foreign languages. They were comfortable bombarding me with questions: How do you eat a sapodilla? Where do dragon fruits grow? How many arms does an octopus have? Why are the eggs black? Their enthusiasm drove me to buy with no exception or hesitation everything that had roused their curiosity. Back at their grandmother's place, we spread the fruit on the garden table before having her sit down with us. To our great surprise, she divided the custard apple in half before eating its milky flesh, spitting the black pits into her hand.

WHEN THE COMMUNISTS WON and the country
was reunified, numerous families were reunited.
Many young people had fled the North by crossing
the seventeenth parallel, which divided the country in
two, leaving behind parents they found again twenty
years later. The young people had become parents in
turn and their children, little Southerners, knew
nothing of the tradition among Northern women of
coating their teeth with black lacquer, an operation
that took two weeks of diligent work by a professional
lacquerer and the same number of days of pain and
discomfort. Jet teeth have been celebrated by the poets
and considered one of the four criteria of women's
beauty. The dye lasted a lifetime and protected the
teeth against any attack by food. Women wore the
shiny black smile with pride until the tradition was
eclipsed by elegance *à la française*. The disappearance
of that cultural legacy was confirmed for me when I
heard a child ask why his grandmother from the
North kept the pits of custard apples in her mouth
instead of spitting them out. The child couldn't
conceive that his grandmother had black-lacquered
teeth and that she was one of the last representatives
of a dying tradition.

I was pleasantly surprised, then, to see Luc's
mother scatter the pits on the table and try unsuccessfully to push one between two others. It was a game
played by Vietnamese children who didn't have
marbles. I approached her to help continue the

măng câu

~

custard apple

movement of her finger, which was refusing to obey her wishes. Luc came to play his turn and, finally, the children. Each one held on jealously to the pits he'd collected and the winner performed a victory dance as if it were the World Cup. They also tried to kneel on the skin of the jackfruit like Vietnamese students being punished, but they jumped as soon as they felt the scales.

While they were playing with wooden swords they'd found when leaving the store, I was caramelizing the fish above a battered, rusty old bucket filled with blazing coals that made it into a kind of grill. I was cooking outside, as they'd done at the orphanage, as is done at most houses in Vietnam. Luc's mother came and sat on a stone beside me, taking the long bamboo chopsticks from my hands to turn the pieces of fish. Luc took her photo so he would never forget that act, which had been absent from his memory for the past twenty-five years. I prepared two portions, one not so spicy, for the children. On the other, Luc's mother sprinkled pepper I'd crushed roughly in a mortar. While we had her attention, I whispered a lie: "The children at the orphanage are well. They can't wait to see you." I don't know if she believed me, but she began stroking my hair again.

I SUGGESTED THAT WE EAT at the children's table
to re-create the atmosphere of the street restaurants in
Vietnam, where the customers sat on very low tables
and stools. Luc's mother was still in the habit of
drinking broth with chrysanthemum leaves after the
fish, at the end of the meal. For dessert, the children
tried unsuccessfully to pick up cubes of mango with
chopsticks. They challenged me, so I placed the pieces
delicately in their mouths, which raised me to the
rank of acrobat or magician. Luc tried to make them
laugh by picking up a cube intended for them. His
abrupt movement sent the cube flying and, instinctively, we both caught it in mid-air. I found myself
one iota from his lips. Until that precise moment, I
had never felt the desire to kiss anyone on the mouth.
As well, when I kissed, I used my nose in the way that
Vietnamese mothers do, inhaling the perfume of milk
from their baby's chubby thighs.

cải cúc

~

chrysanthemum
leaves

hôn

~

kissing

MY HUSBAND AND I didn't exchange kisses as did other couples, either as a greeting or as foreplay. We were still modest, even after two children, even after twenty years of marriage. Language probably contributed to that restraint. We talked about things without naming them. It was enough to say "to be close" (*gần*) to understand that there had been sexual relations. My husband just had to turn towards me and I would understand my wifely duty. It was enough for him to be happy for all of us to be. Our marriage was uneventful, undramatic.

MAMAN HAD TAUGHT ME very early to avoid conflicts, to breathe without existing, to melt into the landscape. Her teachings were essential for my survival, because she was sometimes called away on assignment. We rarely knew when she would leave and even less often when she would come home. While she was away, she sent me to stay with people she knew or who had been ordered to look after me. I learned very quickly to be at once invisible and helpful so that I'd be forgotten, so no one could criticize me, so no one could attack me. I knew exactly when I must set a plate down next to the mother who was on the point of taking the vegetables out of her wok without her seeing my hand, just as I could keep the porcelain filters filled with drinking water with no one seeing me empty the kettles that had cooled down during the night.

I could identify the needs of my foster families in one day, two at most. It was very easy for me, then, to anticipate my husband's wishes before he was aware of them himself. I saw to it that his underwear drawer always held enough white T-shirts with no shoulder seams, a garment worn by certain working-class Chinese. From habit and nostalgia, he had continued to wear one under his shirt. I replaced the worn-out ones with new ones bought in a store in Chinatown without his realizing it because I washed them twice to soften the fabric, to make them his. Similarly, the ball drawer always had new tennis balls for his

vô hình

~

invisible

Wednesday and Friday game nights and more recently, golf balls for Saturday mornings. The advertising inserts were always removed from his *National Geographic*s because those pieces of cardboard irritated him particularly and pointlessly.

As for him, he never criticized me for spending too long in the kitchen, any more than he questioned me about my choices for the children's education. My husband and I were advancing along a road as smooth and level as a landing strip.

LIKE LUC, I HAD A perfect marriage until he
smoothed my hair with the backs of his hands and
breathed in the side of my neck, asking me not to
move or he would fall, he would scream. The only
trace of Luc that I could bring back to Montreal was
that of his hands on my eyes, which he had covered so
that I wouldn't see his tears flow silently in the airport
parking lot. I stood there in front of him, motionless,
overcome by a shock of emotions so foreign to me. He
had watched me cross the security line, leave with no
date and no promise of return.

tóc

~

hair

thở

~

breathe

I LEARNED TO CONTROL my breathing, to need
very little oxygen, like mountain dwellers and those
who lived in the Củ Chi tunnels during the war.
When Maman and I were living in a room assigned
by the government in Hanoi, we slept with a towel
over our noses so we wouldn't be wakened by the foul
smells that came out of the walls like putrid monsters.
In those days, I exhaled more than I inhaled, but I
never suffocated. Through the window, appearing
and disappearing in the clouds, the image of the
fullness of Luc's shoulder under his violet shirt, of his
strong wrist with a red string around it or of his curls
that spilled out of his helmet sucked up all the air in
my lungs and made the enclosed space of the airplane
stifling, unbearable.

ASIDE FROM THE NAIL clipper he kept permanently
in his trouser pocket that I'd used on his sons in his
mother's garden, I still knew nothing about this man
who had suddenly become the centre of my universe,
though I had neither centre nor universe. I may have
been mistaken to have mocked people who believe in
the story of Saint Ông Tơ, whose role is to bind two
persons with love by twining two red silk threads
together between his fingers. Maybe Luc was the red
thread intended for me?

And perhaps he was right after all, the young
student Alexandre, a customer suffering from heart-
break who'd sworn to me one day that he would
never love another and had upheld his conviction by
clipping onto a cord in the window this quotation
from Roland Barthes: "I encounter millions of bodies
in my life; of those millions I may desire hundreds;
but of those hundreds I love only one." At the time,
that sentiment was utterly foreign and incomprehen-
sible to me because I had never experienced that
sensation of exclusivity and uniqueness.

lụa

~

silk

I AM CERTAIN THAT not one passenger had noticed Maman in the crowd in front of the sliding doors on the way out of Customs. To me, she looked particularly thin and old. She seemed to have reached a threshold where she let herself be lulled by time, not in an attitude of surrender but tenderly, as if they were confiding in one another and poking affectionate fun at the whirlwind of youth. Maman stroked the ends of my hair three times, as she'd always done when she came to pick me up from my babysitter. When my hair was short or tied back, I could feel the warmth of her hand on my back, tiny but powerful, like a healer's. I found myself doing the same to my own children when they got off the school bus in front of the house, after a week-long absence. The contrast between the minimalism of my action and the spontaneous affection of Luc's children, who had held me in their arms for an eternity to say goodbye, stunned me.

THE CLOSENESS BETWEEN MY children and Julie has always reassured me. They kissed, embraced, murmured secrets and sweet nothings. Julie took them regularly to concerts, where the conductor would show them how to listen to the instruments to hear the voices of the characters in the stories told in music. She signed them up for hockey, swimming, ballet and drawing. She decided, with my daughter, on her hairstyles: shoulder-length, medium, bangs, no bangs. My children knew Julie's phone number by heart and called her *Má Hai*, Mother Two.

In a family, "Two" expresses the highest rank, and Julie occupied that place because she was older than me, because she was my big sister. Often, the aunts in a family are called "mother" because they have nearly the same duties and the same rights concerning the well-being and education of the child. As soon as Julie came along to guide them, correct them, entertain them, I stepped aside so the relationship between them could deepen and exist without me, after me. In Vietnam, it is said that the fatherless child still eats rice and fish while the motherless child must spread leaves on the ground for sleeping (*Mồ côi Cha ăn cơm với cá; mồ côi Mẹ lót lá mà nằm*). My children were very lucky. They had life insurance and mother insurance.

bảo hiểm

~

insurance

I ALSO THANKED PHILIPPE for telling them constantly, "I love you," with hearts drawn, moulded, written on almond *tuiles*, marshmallows, jujubes or *mousse au chocolat*. My children copied him, spontaneously signing their drawings and cards with hearts, while none of the letters I'd written to Maman contained the three words "I miss you" or mentioned that I suffered from her absence. I had described to her the staggering number of shampoo brands in just one store because I hoped to pour water over her soapy hair again while she bent her head over the aluminum basin that we used for washing clothes.

I had sent her a map of the Metro, explaining the speed of a train plunging into the dark tunnels as precisely as a bullet down the length of the barrel because I preferred the slowness of our train, so slow that we could nearly touch the lives of people who lived near the tracks. The passengers complained at the narrowness of the berths, even in first class, because there were six of us in each compartment. The last berths were attached some thirty centimetres from the ceiling, barely enough room to slip inside. Once, a fat woman had settled in above us, her stomach nearly touching the ceiling. I was terribly afraid that the Formica sheet would break and the woman would land on us, sleeping just underneath. My anxiety soon faded because I was happy to be curled up against Maman. With my nose pressed against the wall, my back covered by her warmth, my head against her heart, I slept the sweetest and deepest of sleeps. Maman thought I must lack air in that limited space, yet I'd never been so alive as during those rare journeys by train, when she protected me against passengers with roaming hands, where she offered me lightness, where she had reduced life and the entire world to a single bubble.

I no longer witnessed, in the window of the house our train nearly touched, the father who threw an iron at his daughter's face because she had on too much makeup. I was no longer listening to the conversation of the two men next to me, reminiscing about their student years in the former Czechoslovakia, how they'd made money clandestinely selling goods that had been rationed. I had stopped counting the cockroaches that zoomed over the walls or wondering if the pink polyester satin pillow, edged with a lot of gathered, dusty flounces, provided by the train, had assembled the entire population of lice in the country. Enclosed in here, I could rest, let myself go and relinquish the millions of details in the world around me. I dismissed everything, knew nothing as soon as I was lying spoon-fashion with Maman.

WHEN LUC'S GAZE WAS ON ME, I had that same impression of exclusion, where the things around me disappeared and the space between us contained my whole life. I had read in a book a client left behind that *regarder*, to look, means *esgarder*, to be considerate, to have *égards* for someone. During the Middle Ages, to describe a state of war or conflict, it was said of enemies: "'Neither one has *regard* for the other.' For centuries the word has contained respect, of course, but also concern, worries for the other." My husband didn't have to offer me either *regard* or *égard* because he didn't need to be anxious on my behalf. Since he often described me to his friends as a woman who would survive as easily in the desert as in Antarctica, he could go on walking and moving away from me without realizing that I was a block behind him, because a strap on my sandal had broken. Since I'd been lucky enough to be chosen by him, by his family, I was the one who should be concerned about him, not the reverse. In any case, I was already seeing to all the details, from the most trivial to the most obvious, from slippers pointing in the right direction by the bed to birthday presents for his family, from the pope's nose of the chicken set aside in his bowl to parents' meetings at the school. I anticipated, I foresaw, I prepared, my hands as invisible as Eleanor Roosevelt's, who filled her husband's fountain pen every morning before putting it back in his jacket pocket.

JEAN-PIERRE, ONE OF our regulars, a paramedic
and former priest, also concerned himself with the
details of the daily life of his Vietnamese wife, Lan,
but always in a festive way. He would lift her in his
arms with the light movement and the supple body of
a dancer. He had seen her at the same time on the
same Metro platform for four days before he
approached her, smiling. In front of his big blue-green
eyes, she had frozen like a deer in the headlights. She
was one of those women Mother Nature had
neglected or who, on the contrary, had been created to
confirm the existence of sublimated love. Lan had
always behaved as if she were invisible, to avoid
intrusive eyes. She carried an umbrella in her purse to
hide from the sun, snow, rain and people, and indoors
she would disappear behind an open book.

Jean-Pierre had noticed the French exercise book
given to adult immigrants, which she was reading
assiduously. He had greeted her with a word or two
before he held out the restaurant's card with a hand-
written hour and date. He had asked me to write on
the back that I would be his interpreter. She had
phoned me before the date of the appointment. She
assumed it was a trap, but Jean-Pierre only wanted to
tell her that she was as beautiful as the Blessed Virgin
and that he would like to take care of her. At first,
Jean-Pierre waited patiently for her at the entrance to
the Metro, walking a few steps behind so he wouldn't
scare her, and gradually he'd approached her to

Đức Mẹ

~

Blessed Virgin

relieve her of a bag weighed down with dictionaries. And then, one day, he had asked her to marry him, had sponsored her parents, her two brothers and her four sisters, had made a garden for her and reserved a wall for photos of her in winter, in love, in the family way . . . To us, he had presented her beauty like a French jeweller convincing his customers of the magnificence of an uncut diamond. Lan had never dreamed that a hand would caress her cheeks ravaged by adolescence—nor had she planned her departure from Nha Trang.

She had ended up by chance one night in the middle of a group disembarking silently and swiftly from a truck covered with canvas and now heading for a plank joining the shore to a boat. She had been taken there by the hasty movement of a hundred persons, with whom she had reached the shores of Indonesia and, some years later, the island of Montreal. Chance had given her a new beginning and a love that erased the grey of her teeth, damaged by tetracycline, and had softened her skeletal silhouette that her neighbours called "dried squid," a delicacy sold on the beach whose flesh was flattened and hung by a thread in the sunlight like clothing on a rope, with no body. Jean-Pierre had discreetly wrapped that bony structure with his flesh by standing close to her, always. Whenever I saw Lan, during the first seconds, I was always surprised at the gap between her and my impression of her, that of a dazzling woman.

WHEN I CAME HOME FROM PARIS, my face may
have given me away. Maman had grasped my fever-
ishness at once, despite the flood of presents on the
living room table: ribbons for my daughter's hair; a
big book with photos of French army planes, a subject
that fascinated my son; marrons glacés, a stupendous
delight for my husband, who had discovered them
when an aunt who lived in Niort brought some to his
parents. For Maman I had some of the Seyès ruled
notebooks like those she'd used as a child, on which
the *l*s all stopped at the fourth horizontal line and
the round of the *o*s was restricted to the first two. I'd
bought ten, hoping she would write our story, hers
and mine before she was mine, and that she would
leave her words as a legacy for my children.

The night of my return, I fell asleep at the same
time they did, before my husband, which allowed me
to get up in the middle of the night and read and
reread the dozen emails Luc had sent to describe Paris
without me. He had followed my plane, kilometre by
kilometre, hour by hour, cloud by cloud. I went and
sat in the kitchen plunged in darkness, where Maman
came and found me, not saying a word. She brought
me tea and a box of tissues, and we stayed like that
until sunrise, until the first rustlings of bedclothes.

OVER THE WEEKS THAT followed my return, Luc
constructed a new universe for me with words that
were hardly ever spoken, such as "my angel," which
became exclusively mine. In my mind, I now heard
only his voice, asking what was new every morning
at 8:06, the hour when I started my day's work.
At the same time, catering orders were multiplying,
which justified my solitary nights in the kitchen
cutting lengthwise fine slices of lotus root the size
of a straw, and counting for Luc the number of holes
in the young shoots. He would listen to me on the
telephone as if he were attending a recital. I sometimes asked his opinion on the passages I chose to
write on the back of menus for private evenings.

Once, for a fundraiser, I went back to an old
Chinese lesson where the teacher had explained that
the character for the verb "to love" incorporated three
ideograms: a hand, a heart and a foot, because we must
express our love while holding our heart in our hand
as we walk to the beloved and make our offering. Julie
had printed the explanation on long sheets of red
paper that my children, Maman, and the daughters of
Hồng and of Julie had sewn onto the bodies of hundreds of origami cranes. In the function room, birds
suspended from the ceiling came down to the guests to
deliver this message, which I had originally addressed
to Luc. His crane was covered with words that I'd
adopted as a second skin so I could identify the brand
new feelings that were tormenting me. In reaction to

my half-avowed declaration, Luc had sent me an official invitation to a festival at which restaurant owners would entertain a foreign chef in their kitchens for a week. Clients would be offered three evenings when unfamiliar knowledge and expertise would be wed.

Not knowing Luc's true motivation, everyone was happy about this Parisian showcase—everyone but Maman, who reminded me that success attracts thunderbolts, which was why particularly beautiful newborns were given hideous names. Parents would call them such things as "dwarf" or "gnome" or "corkscrew" (a reference to a pig's tail), and families tricked the gods by referring to them as ugly, loathsome, forgettable. Otherwise, they'd have attracted the attention of jealous wandering spirits, capable of casting evil spells.

I TOO TRIED TO FOOL myself by thinking of my encounter with Luc as a tragedy, a drama or a calamity that had swallowed me whole. Had I been a zealous Catholic, I would have worn a hair shirt and practised mortification for self-denial, so as to kill this sudden desire to live, to live to a great age. I heard mothers dream, make plans to attend their children's graduations, their weddings, the births of grandchildren. Unlike them, I could never imagine those different points of arrival, those different milestones that punctuated their road. My role was limited to that of a bridge or a ferryman who would help them ford a river or cross a border, with no wish to follow them to the end. My movements had always been dictated by the humdrum life of every day, by Maman's missions, by impossibilities and possibilities. Like her, I had never chosen one particular goal. Yet somehow here I was seated once again on an airplane taking me towards a precise destination, planned, desired, and most of all towards a person who was waiting for me, who would welcome me, take me in.

AT THE AIRPORT'S TERMINAL 3, Luc did not
appear when the doors opened, which matched one of
the many scenarios I had anticipated. Instinctively, my
hand had started searching my purse for the notebook
on which I'd jotted the telephone number of a cousin
of Maman's who'd been living in a suburb of Paris
since the late fifties.

 I had visited her on my last trip. She and her
husband were frozen in revolutionary Vietnam. He
wore the Communist soldiers' green cap as he was
digging in his garden like a farmer, and she, in black
trousers and dark shirt, was washing some freshly
picked cherries for me by rubbing them together one
by one as if she were still in Vietnam, where herbs and
lettuces had to be sterilized with potassium perman-
ganate that turned the water purple. She had brought
out some old letters from Maman, with whom she'd
corresponded regularly until Maman disappeared.
She wrote to her in Vietnamese and Maman replied
in French. The two women were the same age and
the cousin had been Maman's confidante during the
difficult years with her "cold mother." Maman had
given me her name and contact information with no
other explanation except for a brief sentence on a card
without an envelope: "Sister, this is my daughter. I'll
explain someday."

THAT COUSIN, WHO'D BECOME an aging hunchback, took my photo to add to the family history, with an old camera protected by its leather case. She promised to send the photos to us and I promised to do the same with pictures of Maman and my children. I knew that I could turn up at her house without notice like the last time, like in Vietnam, where doors were opened without knowing who would be there.

Maman and I had showed up suddenly at Sister Two's house one day without a word in advance. Maman had resurfaced to save her from imminent danger.

SISTER TWO WAS MARRIED to a retired high-rank-
ing official in the old political regime, which turned
her into an enemy of the people under Communism.
At the time, one needed only live on a large property
to be subjected to a variety of accusations. Sister Two's
family corresponded to the portrait of capitalists guilty
not only of the country's decline but also of its devas-
tation and its indecency. After an absence of more
than twenty years, Maman had rung the bell and
Sister Two had received her and settled her into the
house as if the absence had been only physical; or that
time had accounted for her absence; or that the
wrinkles on their faces were already recounting their
respective lives lived in the other's absence.

Thanks to her status as participant in the revolu-
tion, Maman had been able to prevent the family's
expulsion into hostile zones to clear the land and dig
canals with shovel in hand and only rations of barley
to eat. No one then could compare those arid and
hostile territories with the ones in Siberia because
most likely no one would survive in either place,
according to the revenants who slept in the street,
often on the sidewalk in front of their former home.
I wondered if it would be unbearable to have your
past planted right in front of you. Maybe they hoped
that out of compassion the new occupants would
take them in, give them back a corner of the house,
so that the past would no longer be a flaw, so that
people would no longer have to take a felt pen to

chính trị

~

politics

erase controversial faces and flags of the old regime on photos, and, above all, to reintegrate the past into the present.

WHILE I WAS GROPING in my purse for the address book, from the corner opposite the airport exit I saw a man running towards me. In less than a second his face appeared, and at that exact moment I was in the present tense; a present without a past. He had stood off to one side to observe my arrival, to test us, to measure his resistance, which had lasted exactly seventeen seconds. An eternity, he had said, adding: *"C'est l'évidence"*—It's obvious.

In my circle, I often heard the expression, *C'est pas évident*—It's not obvious!—but never the opposite, and always as an adjective. As a common noun, I knew only the English definition that talks about proofs, or "a body of facts," that confirm or contradict a belief or that help draw a conclusion. Between French and English, such *faux amis*—false friends— set their traps and every time, I fall in.

Luc knew that I committed millions of errors in grammar and logic, but also in comprehension. Like a sherpa, he guided me through the bends and curves, the twists and turns of the French language, undressing it layer by layer, one subtlety at a time, like stripping a rose of its petals. And so the meaning of the word *évidence* was explained to me, underlined and expressed in a hundred different ways, in contexts as varied as they were unexpected.

In his opinion, it was the *évidence* that had shown him the hooks hidden behind the buckles on the straps of my pumps, because his hands had taken

quá khú

~

past

them off without hesitating, as if he'd rehearsed that action all his life. It was the obvious as well that had made me feel entitled to place my lips in the hollow of his collarbones and to elect it as my resting place. For the first time I felt the urge to plant my flag in that square centimetre and to declare it mine, whereas Maman and I had left so many places without even glancing behind us. If it weren't for the obvious, we would have seen the sun set over the city and I'd have recited to him the poem by Edwin Morgan.

> When you go,
> if you go,
> and I should want to die,
> there's nothing I'd be saved by
> more than the time
> you fell asleep in my arms
> in a trust so gentle,
> I let the darkening room
> drink up the evening, till
> rest, or the new rain
> lightly roused you awake.
> I asked if you heard the rain in your dream,
> and half-dreaming still you only said, I love you.

LUC FELL ASLEEP BESIDE ME even though he'd
never before given himself over to sleep in a lover's
arms. As for me, I had learned how to fall asleep very
quickly, on command, so that my eyelids would serve
as curtains over landscapes or scenes from which I
preferred to be absent. I was able to move from
consciousness to unconsciousness with a snap of the
fingers, between two sentences, or before the remark
that would offend me was spoken. Oddly enough,
during that day stolen from time, I couldn't sleep. I
engraved in my memory every fragment of Luc's
skin. I counted each of the folds in his body, including those in his neck, in the cubital fossa, that reverse
of the elbow, and the popliteal cavity, the *H* just
behind the knees—all the grooves where dirt lodged
when I was a child.

Mothers had to scrub those spots that imprisoned
dust carried by the wind and caught unintentionally
by children. Observing the lines of Luc's body, I
realized that I'd never had a chance to run my fingers
over my children's folds because they never came
home with collars of dirt, as I did after a day of school.
The Montreal air must have been filtered, purified—
or was it simply too pure to leave traces? The whiteness of Luc's skin bore that purity, even though the
scar above his eye told of his closeness with his dog
and the one on his ankle, of his reckless youth, a mark
that still made him jump at the slightest touch.

THE PAINLESS SCAR on my thigh showed skin burned by the hot water in a Thermos bottle spilled, accidentally most likely, by a child who was afraid of having to share the powdered milk I was stirring up in a glass for her. Maman had never seen that burn, only the scar when she returned from far-off places, whose names could not be spoken of.

I hadn't seen her wound either, only the hole from the bullet that had pierced her right calf. She'd reassured me, saying it had been an accident. I had reassured her in turn, saying it was my own awkwardness. We never had to talk about those scars again, because Maman didn't wear skirts and I didn't wear minis. My husband assumed it was a birthmark, and my children saw no anomaly because I didn't parade around the pool in a swimsuit, never stretched out on the beach to melt in the sun. Only Luc had observed that slight discoloration of my skin long enough to make out a map of the world there and to draw the road he would walk along towards me. Meanwhile, he had to attend a parents' meeting with his wife, at the children's school, far from me.

I LISTENED FOR HIS FOOTFALL on the first steps before I ran to the balcony. He came back into the bedroom and found me leaning over the banister, on tiptoe, waiting for his silhouette to appear on the sidewalk. I went down to his car with him so that he would leave, so that he would continue to be a good father. I reminded him that he wasn't abandoning me, that the bed still held the shape of his back and the pillow, that of his arm which had reached for me after the brief moment when he'd nodded off. I was sitting a breath away from him, just far enough to watch over his sleep without disturbing him.

I had learned to glide silently both inside and outside the covers because my husband was a very light sleeper. Early in our first months together, he had asked me to sew for him a long, round cushion like the one he used to wrap his arms and legs around when he was a child. Only that human-size cushion could soothe him and keep him from dreaming about his grandfather who often, in the middle of the night, gathered together in the ancestors' hall the grandchildren and children who lived on the family property so that all would kneel before him and listen to him scolding his wife. The grandfather imposed his authority on the house just as he did on the military base. He demanded absolute obedience so he could go on giving orders that would rip open the sky and tear apart destinies in the hundreds without blinking, without collapsing. My husband slept with frayed nerves. A single clumsy movement on my part and he would waken with a start, frightened eyes staring at me, surprised I was there. Luc had had the same terrified expression when he'd felt, unconsciously, not my presence but my absence.

ON THE NIGHTS WHEN WE offered the Vietnamese
menu, Luc set up three islands in the restaurant. The
first held huge platters of woven water hyacinth filled
with fresh herbs for preparing spring rolls, and green
papaya salad with dried beef marinated in rice wine,
wrapped in sesame seeds and grilled at a very low
temperature for ten hours. Two young Vietnamese
girls in silk smocks slit to the waist on both sides
handled the rolls with the slowness of hot countries
and the confidence of young girls in bloom.

Luc had decorated the second island with four
yoke baskets containing bowls, rice noodles and two
big cauldrons of broth, including one typical of Hue,
the former imperial capital that took pride in the
refinement of its cuisine, conceived and developed for
emperors and dignitaries.

The third was reserved for me, for turning crepes
with turmeric, pork and shrimp, a process that
required a flexible wrist and quick movements so the
batter would cover both the bottom and the walls of
the pan, in a thin layer. Since the name of the dish—
bánh xèo—evokes the sound of the liquid crackling in
contact with the heat, the temperature had to be high
but controlled to prevent it from boiling. The challenge was to stuff the crepe with bean sprouts and
yellow beans and fold it in two without breaking it. It
always pained me to break the first finished crepe, but
I had no trouble with the one offered to Luc. I
wanted him to taste the pleasure of feeling the crepe

xèo

~

pschiii!

give way and crack between his lips. I could feel the fine crust melting in his mouth and disappearing instantly, as fast as the beating of wings. And I hurried to wrap the second mouthful with a leaf of white mustard so it would leave a hint of bitterness and freshness on his tongue.

DURING SERVICE, I WOULD see him going from table to table trying to persuade diners to use their hands for the crepes, which were at once majestic and so fragile. Even if the place was packed, looking up from the three crackling woks for even half a second would inevitably make me lock eyes with Luc, who would be opening a bottle of wine at a distant table or greeting a faithful customer at the entrance. I recognized myself in those eyes as I'd have recognized myself in the mirror on our bedroom wall, where we had stopped time. I had only a few mirrors in my house in Montreal, one too high, one too hidden away, and a tiny one my husband had hung at the front door to drive away evil spirits. Like them, who are terrified by their own reflection, I jumped whenever I saw mine because it didn't correspond with the image I had of myself. Yet next to Luc's face, mine resembled me, like something obvious. If I were a photo, Luc would be the developer and the fixer of my face, which until that day existed only in negative.

gương
~
mirror

AT THE END OF THAT STAY, I cried for six hours in the horrible airplane cutting me off from him, from us, from me. I had lost my footing three times during the journey between airport and home . . . a step too high, a door too small, a word too long. Luckily, I arrived in the usual hubbub of every day: homework, dance class, hockey practice, restaurant. Life caught me when I fell and Luc's letter on the desk in the workshop helped me regain my equilibrium. In the envelope, one sentence: "You have arrived," written inside a pencil tracing of his left hand. He had sent it the day after I arrived in Paris, hoping it would cushion my landing in Montreal.

Over the next days and weeks, he sent me photos: of the street where he'd stopped to help an old lady lift her grocery bag off the sidewalk; of a newly installed doorknob; of a café table outside a refinery bordered by poppies in the background. We had tried to be ubiquitous by fitting our worlds together and moving the continents. We drew up scenarios for preventing the tornado that was engulfing us from ravaging the land and destroying the nests that we'd built, twig by twig, over nearly two decades.

ON MY BIRTHDAY, a date Maman had chosen at random in the office where birth certificates were issued, Luc gave me a gift of twenty-four hours. He came to join me in Quebec City, where I was giving a culinary workshop. We spent the night measuring again and again his long femur against mine; counting the number of kisses it took to cover my body compared with his; and, above all, making fun of my impatience for his arrival. I had burst out of my hiding place behind the dressing gown hanging in the bathroom as soon as I heard the click of the door. Without a run-up, I flew into his arms.

Julie once took me to a class where one of the exercises consisted of climbing a ladder and falling backwards, to be caught in the arms of the other members of the group. I'd tried several times, in vain. If I were to do it again now, I would lean back eyes closed, with the same heedlessness that had allowed my body to collapse against Luc's.

I am still angry with myself for having dozed off several times during that night, as if a life together were already established before us, entire and possible. I think Luc spent a sleepless night, because every time I half-opened my eyes, my gaze was met by his, waiting for it with the tenderness of certainty. At dawn, we went outside to smell the dew and the aroma of carrot muffins, my favourites except for the *tarte Bourdaloue* with pears and pistachios that we'd sampled together on the steps of St. Eustache church in Paris.

He left again the following afternoon, asking me to sew one of my hairs into the weave of his jacket and another into the bottom of the right-hand pocket of his jeans. On the station platform, he wrote on my palm that he promised to love the cold and the whiteness of sheets that mattered so much to me. And then, with no warning, he got down from the train to announce that he would take a taxi to give us half an hour more, and also to plan my return to France in response to an invitation from two restaurant owners in the countryside.

THAT VISIT AND THEN two more gave me time to
kiss and baptize each of Luc's beauty marks with the
name of a place where we would exist without
wounding any family or friends, our first raisons
d'être. I counted each of those ruby spots as attentively
and proudly as most Vietnamese, who conferred on
them the role of good luck charms and saw them as
precious because they were so rare on dark skin. I
showed him the yellow colour of my palm and he
talked to me about the *grain*, or texture, of my
imberbe, or smooth-cheeked, skin, two words Luc had
added to my vocabulary by placing them next to
dependence and *gluttony*, old terms that had been given
a whole new meaning.

ruồi son

~

birthmarks

va-li

~

suitcase

THE LAST TIME WE SAW each other in Paris, when we were hastily closing my suitcase, Luc asked: "If I showed up at your door next week, what would you say?" Instinctively, without even taking the time to stop what I was doing, I replied with one word, "Disaster," kissing him. It was a real question and I hadn't understood it.

I DIDN'T KNOW THAT a lot of tears had flowed at his house, that unspeakable words had been flung and wounds inflicted. When I finally grasped the scope of his question and the impact of my reply, it was already too late. The final nail had been driven into the lid of my coffin when his wife, without reproaching me, announced her intention on the phone: "I'm staying. Do you understand? I am staying."

I received that declaration when I was preparing red snappers to be steamed with ten condiments (*cá chưng*) for a wedding anniversary party. On the work table, vermicelli, cat's ear mushrooms, shiitakes, soya beans in brine, minced pork, finely grated strands of carrot and ginger, sliced peppers: everything was ready but the lilies. I knotted them one by one so the petals wouldn't come undone while they were being cooked. That repetitive act allowed me to hear in my head Luc's voice whispering sentimental songs without anyone being aware. I was absolutely not expecting that call from his wife, which petrified me. I remember seeing my hands continue to remove the pistils from the flowers, to garnish the fish and place them in the enormous *bain-marie* with the big holes, but I've forgotten the rest, what came next.

đinh

~

nail

MAMAN HAD BEEN EDUCATED by Catholic nuns all through her childhood. She knew a lot of stories from the Bible that she would tell me to back up a message or a lesson. That night, I took charge of cleaning and closing the kitchen. She stayed with me and slipped in the story of the Judgment of Solomon before disappearing up the stairs.

I washed the kitchen floor on my knees, holding a scrub brush and weeping profusely. I sharpened the knives on the whetstone. I went out back with a flashlight and removed the wilted flowers and dead leaves from the garden. And most important, I held my breath—to cut myself in half, to amputate Luc from me, to die partially. Otherwise, he would die entirely, torn in two, in seven, in shreds, making his children into collateral injured.

MY SAFE HAVEN LAY IN cooking elaborate, time-consuming dishes. Julie supported me in these extravagant projects by lightening my schedule and cutting down on my usual tasks without my knowledge. For Tết, the Vietnamese New Year, I spent nights at a time boning chickens without tearing the skin, then stuffing and sewing them up. I also gave the local Buddhist temple a large plant covered with mandarin oranges hung one by one on the branches. Each fruit had a wish wrapped around its stem, intended for the one who would pick it on the stroke of midnight. For the Moon Festival in August, I made *bánh trung thu*, mid-autumn moon cakes that the Vietnamese savour while they watch the children walking down the street with their red lanterns lit by candles. The fillings vary according to taste and the time we spend on them.

I had all of eternity because time is infinite when we don't expect anything. And so I had decided on a stuffing with many kinds of roasted nuts and watermelon seeds that I husked by cracking the tough bark of each one very firmly. To avoid touching the delicate flesh inside required a lot of control to stop at the right moment. Otherwise, the flesh would break like a dream on waking. It was painstaking work that allowed me to withdraw into my own universe, the one that no longer existed.

Fortunately, there are no verb tenses in the Vietnamese language. Everything is said in the infinitive, in the present tense. It was easy, then, to forget to add "tomorrow," "yesterday" or "never" to my sentences to make Luc's voice ring out.

I had the impression that we had lived a lifetime together. I could visualize precisely the position of his right forefinger pointing up when he was annoyed, his body relaxed in the shadow of the shutters, the way he wrapped his long royal blue scarf around his neck when he was running after his children.

LUC'S ABSENCE HAD LED to the disappearance not
only of himself and of "us," but of a large part of
myself as well. I had lost the woman who laughed
like a teenager when she tasted the ten flavours of
sorbet at the oldest ice-cream maker in Paris, as well
as the one who dared to look at herself lingeringly in
a mirror to decipher the reflection of the word
written in felt pen on her back. Today, when I stand
on a stepstool at the bathroom mirror, I can sometimes find the blurry remains of the letters *ruoma* if I
read from the top of my spine to the bottom and
amour in the opposite direction.

I don't recall exactly how much time passed before
Maman intervened. In the absolute dark of her
bedroom, where she had asked me to spend the night,
she put a small metal plate the size of a tea biscuit into
my hand. It was one of the two dog tags belonging to
Phương, the young boy who'd become a soldier and
who had given her a poem when she was a teenager.
The tags embossed with the same essential information about him had to be worn around his neck at all
times, unless he fell on the battlefield and a comrade
in arms pulled one off to take back to the base. Before
he left, he'd gone to see her in uniform and given her
the plate to offer her "the life he hadn't lived" and his
dream of her that would be eternally a dream if he
didn't come back to retrieve it.

For many years, every time Maman saw a military
helmet abandoned by the side of a rice paddy or in

thẻ bài

~

dog tags

some reeds, turned right or wrong side out, empty or filled with rainwater, she thought she would collapse from inside. If her feet hadn't been obliged to continue advancing in her comrades' footprints, she'd have knelt beside those helmets and never got up again. Fortunately, the silence of the single file kept her upright, for a false move could trigger a mine, endangering the lives of all those soldiers ready to stop the cannons from sliding down a muddy slope by lying in front of the wheels: sacrificing themselves for the cause of a nation.

WHEN SHE CAME BACK from the jungle, she went to find Phương, who lived in the family house with his aging parents and his child, who was still at his mother's breast. He had become a doctor, a man respected and loved, according to the people in the village. She had observed him settle down for the noonday siesta in his hammock in the shade of the coconut palms. Bare-chested, shirt hanging on a branch, army chain still around his neck. She had watched him sleep and wake. She had expected him to get up when he moved his arm, but he had stayed motionless amid the rustling of leaves and the plashing of the tails of the carp in the pond. It was in that peaceful, everyday calm that she had noticed Phương's hand hunt for the clasp on the chain wrapped with ribbon that she'd removed from her hair to give him on the night he left. The ribbon was not satin like those of her young half-sisters, because she'd had to create it by weaving and twisting very tightly the hundreds of bits of embroidery thread her stepmother had thrown out.

Maman made Phương's head turn not by advancing towards him but by walking two steps away from him. She stood with her back to him until he left for his medical clinic. Out of love, she never returned.

NEITHER MAMAN NOR I slept that night. The next day, I fixed the children's breakfast as I did every morning, as quietly as possible so as not to waken my husband, who preferred his mornings to be calm and solitary. I handed them their lunch boxes on the doorstep as I did every day, but that morning I sensed Luc's hand stroking my upper back so that I would bend down to their level and kiss them, as he would have done if he'd been there, as he did with his own children every morning.

And two days later, I slipped a tiny note into their sandwich wrappings, the same one Luc wrote to me at the end of every message, like a signature: "I love you, my angel."

Since then, I comb my daughter's hair with the same movements as Luc, who cherished each strand of mine. In the same way, I apply cream to my son's back, stroking the nape of his neck.

Then, one afternoon, with Julie by my side, I went to see the Vietnamese beautician who had told me that her clients claimed she had the power to thwart destiny and give them new fates by tattooing red beauty marks in strategic spots recommended by "destiny readers."

ON MY FIRST VISIT, I had a red dot tattooed at the edge of my forehead, a centimetre to the left of my nose. I made a second appointment for a second mark at the top of my inner right thigh on the day I needed a reason to look at the blue sky and wait to see the trail of a plane. The third time, it was in honour of the leaf of a Japanese maple found by chance between two pages of a dictionary that Luc had sent along with the ring we had chosen together. There was an interior garden in the jewellery store, home to the miniature tree. The owner had allowed Luc to take a leaf when he went there a month later to pick up the ring that had been adjusted to fit my finger. The fourth time, it was snowing very lightly. A large flake settled on the tip of my nose that morning, in the same place where Luc had taken another one away with his lips.

Those visits to the beautician allowed me to reproduce on my body those red dots of Luc's that I knew by heart. I think that on the day when I have all those red dots tattooed, if I were to join them, I would be drawing the map of his destiny on my body. And maybe on that day he will show up at my door, take me by the hand as he always did instinctively, and stop me from saying "Disaster" as he kisses me.

yên lặng

~

silence

PERMISSIONS

Grateful acknowledgement is made to the following
for permission to reprint previously published
material:

Page 11: From *Cửa đã mở, Thơ* by Việt Phương,
2008.

Page 18: Nguyễn Du, lines 1–8.

Page 80: Rumi, *Bridge to the Soul*, translator
Coleman Barks. Copyright © 2007 by Coleman
Barks. Reprinted by permission of HarperCollins
Publishers.

Page 118: Edwin Morgan, *New Selected Poems*,
Carcanet Press, Manchester, 2000.

KIM THÚY has worked as a seamstress, interpreter, lawyer and restaurant owner. She currently lives in Montreal, where she devotes herself to writing.

SHEILA FISCHMAN is the award-winning translator of some 150 contemporary novels from Quebec. In 2008 she was awarded the Molson Prize in the Arts. She is a Member of the Order of Canada and a chevalier of the Ordre national du Québec. She lives in Montreal.

A NOTE ABOUT THE TYPE

The main text of *Mān* is set in Granjon, a modern
recutting of a typeface derived from the classic
letterforms of Claude Garamond (1480-1561). It is
named in honour of Robert Granjon, a successful
sixteenth-century French publisher, punch cutter and
founder, and a contemporary of Garamond.

Display text is set in Linotype Didot.